The Violinist

or "Once More, Without Feeling"

a novel by

Royce Grubic

ISBN: 0615490255
ISBN 13: 978-0615490250

contents

1: chelsea, darlene, dolores   1

2: patrick, gertrude, rose   9

3: nero, farza, cleosutra   15

4: jake, darren, aunt amy   22

5: manny, grandpa, noah   29

6: wolfgang, god   35

7: hate   40

8: norman bates   44

9: the orchestra   47

10: carrie and jerry   51

11: jenny, sierra, and lance   61

12: death and the maiden   69

13: skippy   74

14: po boy   82

15: shitheads   91

16: yo einstein and omygod jack   98

17: sibelius, huck finn, filbert   109

18: frodo, fonzie, j. edgar   120

19: girls   130

20: flirp and blerf, robert frost and merv   146

21: sock hops, not much   157

22: squirrelgate   180

23: descartes   196

24: matinee   207

25: so long, space captain   214

26: ebola joe   226

27: jenny revisited   237

28: headlock   246

29 (epilogue): the end of the affair   250

composed during the spring and summer of 2008
moscow, idaho

chapter one

chelsea, darlene, dolores

After closing time at the mall . . . there is an eerie quiet, which is the sixth best kind of quiet. An indoor dusk has fallen over the Sunglass Hut. The metal grated storefront gates have all been slammed down and safely locked. Big hair tumbleweeds drift across the atrium floor. Orange Julius has left the building. Does anyone know Chelsea is here? She sits unseen for now, silent, until such time as a pot-bellied security guard, murmuring janitor, or wayward ghost might happen by. Soon, probably.

A busy month it's been. Lazing in a rainforest of plastic plants (the filigree of fake tropical leaves), Chelsea reflects on her

1

killing spree. First of all, it's the sheer fault of *spree* for rhyming so conveniently and happily with fun words like *glee* and *whee!* and . . . *flee*. Spree clearly has an outstanding pedigree in this regard — well, aside from *pee* and *stung by a bee*. Neither a "pee spree" nor "bee sting spree" seem all that inviting, true. But a killing spree, how could Chelsea resist? Especially when it was such a financially solid business venture. And you can't spell adventure without venture. Or vent.

Or dent.

The idea first occurred to her while performing an adagio dirge version of "Come on Eileen" at a funeral service here in town. Or better said, it first occurred to Darlene, the spry little dark-haired devil on Chelsea's shoulder, who suddenly spoke up.

"Psst . . . hey, Chelsea! Chelsea!!!"

"What?"

Darlene could tell by Chelsea's tone that she should lower her voice to a discreet whisper. "Hey, this is easy money, huh? Easy. What are you making, like $100 for five minutes of fiddlin'?"

"Mmm." She hated it when Darlene called it fiddlin'. Fiddling was for hillbillies and one-legged pirates. Chelsea was

2

a *violinist.*

"$100 for five minutes! Jeez, that's more than prostitutes — even those fancy high-class 'gentleman's escorts', and a lot more than those cheapo rent-a-skanks. That's $1200 an hour! You could totally clean up doing this. Look at them," Darlene said as she pointed out to the sullen funeral attendees. "There's not a dry eye in the house. They *love* it."

"And?" Despite the distracting conversation with Darlene, Chelsea was a polished enough violinist to continue playing the song beautifully, or at least was skilled enough to conceal the fact that she was no longer entirely "in" the moment. To the untrained eye and ear, it was all the same.

"Think about it," Darlene continued, "let's say you do a hundred funerals at $100 a pop, that's . . . "

"A thousand dollars!" Chelsea said after a moment, now interested. Darlene was much better at math than Chelsea, however, as is so often the case with shoulder devils and devils in general.

"Um, no, Chels, it's *ten thousand* dollars."

"Wow!" she responded with the lilting voice of someone who has caught the drift. Her eyes widened. "That's like three months if I do one per day. So what are you saying, that I should advertise for more funeral gigs? I could make flyers! I have that new pack of sparkly markers!"

"Well, you could do that, sure, go crazy, but what we *really* need . . . and I mean really . . . is a steady supply of stiffs. In this game, sweetie, it appears that corpses equal cash. Especially . . . especially if there is no partner to split the dough with." Darlene slithered closer to Chelsea's ear. "No partner means two hundred."

Chelsea was dutifully accompanied in this particular performance by Gerald, a fifteen year-old accordion prodigy. She glanced at him methodically squeezing the ribs of that dying animal between his pale skinny arms and would hardly call him a "partner." No Gerald would mean twice as much money for her, 47 fewer pimples in the world, one less colony of backne, and many fewer awkward moments for humankind. Although accordionists tend to be conspicuous and don't so easily disappear, she thought, that could be a problem . . .

"C'mon, are you with me?"

"Shh!" Chelsea answered audibly and angrily, glaring at Darlene, just barely sliding her fingers off of a bad note in time. This exchange was fortunately drowned out by the wails and sobs of the gathered mourners, which had risen in their combined anguish to levels worthy of a Sophoclean chorus, intensified by the music. Gerald looked over in momentary curiosity, gave her a clumsy pubescent smile and then returned to his soulful pumping. One, two, three, four; one, two, three, four . . .

♪ ♪ ♪

The mini-concerto now over, Chelsea sat on the front step of the funeral home waiting for her ride home, deep in thought, as was Darlene, nested on Chelsea's shoulder, as was the devil on Darlene's shoulder (Dolores), and so on, exponentially, all the micro-devils and nano-devils ad infinitum. Wasn't it Saint Augustine or one of those other heavenly shitheads who asked how many angels can dance on a head of a pin? If you ask me, I'd rather watch devils dance, that dirty sultry sweaty dancing with the pounding bass, *thoop thoop thud thud*. But there was no dancing, just the heavy silence of an idea being seriously entertained — *seriously*. A seed had been planted.

That night, wrapped warmly in her quilt cocoon, Chelsea's mind drifted along with the shadows on the wall as she contemplated the ins and outs of the emergent scheme. She had no doubts at all about her ability to concoct and execute the proverbial perfect crime—that wasn't the issue. *Murder is such a dirty word* is the thing. Dirty dirty. For starters she would need a much more friendly euphemism, like "expedited expiration" or "assisted non-living" or "death coaching." She soon settled on a favorite: *express shipping*.

She remembered the Ten Commandments and "Thou shalt not kill" but couldn't recall anything specific about "thou shalt not assist to not live" or "thou shalt not death coach." Well, not in any of the parts she had read, which wasn't a lot. There were all those begats and battles and the pages upon pages where God yells at everybody and shoots lightning out of his pits. Plus the Crusaders were Christians, the cream of the crop, and they killed old women and babies and raped chickens, right? (Of course, she had to admit, they were marching around in 120-degree heat wearing suits of armors and pots and pans on their heads, so not exactly the best role models.) And hadn't God Himself in his Divine Effulgent Glory express-shipped the citizens of Sodom and Gomorrah to a fiery grave, just for things that every ten year old today has seen a thousand times on the internet? And what about those poor bastards He drowned so divinely while he let Noah sail away scot-free on his animal kingdom boat party? Can anyone say "bestiality," huh? (And does the expression "scot-free" have something to do with kilts?) Hell, God dispatched Job's first family and gave the dude a screaming case of the shingles, all just because He was suckered into a bet with Satan that blameless ol' Job wouldn't lose his faith. Killing is evidently God's way of spreading his Word, Chelsea concluded. Like bloody butter. Harmgerine. If anything, she was becoming *more* religious as this lovely plan came together.

As Chelsea lay in bed, she began making a list in her mind of top candidates to be expedited to the afterworld. Those frat guys and sorority whores would be perfect, she thought, since they are all basically clones anyway. No one would really notice for a while, and someone would make more soon enough. In a pinch, just put a baseball hat on a side of beef or slab of concrete, there you have one ersatz frat guy. To give him a sorority sis and companion, one need only roll out a few alcohol-soaked mannequins with blonde wigs and over-stretched orifices. Fill the cavity where the brain would be with cosmetics and jizz. Hmm . . . but while easy to lure, frat guys tend to be athletic and big and thus their dead bodies would be hard to lug around. And sorority girls usually appear in gaggles and never alone . . . so if she were going to express ship one she'd have to express ship, um, like, y'know, *omygod,* ten. And would there actually be a demand for violin music at their funerals, or just tape-recorded versions of Christina Aguilera singing John Lennon's "Imagine"? "Be realistic, Chelsea," she reprimanded herself. As much as they all deserve to die, it would have to wait for a more appropriate and experienced express shipper.

No, given her physical limitations and aversion to non-euphemistic killing, what made the most sense would be a steady campaign of aggressive plug-pulling and occasional smothering. "Aha, the Nursing Home!" That settled, Chelsea drifted off into a good night's sleep, with peaceful dreams about painted turtles, unchlorinated swimming pools, orange sherbet, and absolutely no screaming bunnies.

chapter two
patrick, gertrude, rose

Day 1 of the spree just happened to be St. Patrick's Day. Chelsea wore an electric blue blouse, slightly faded jeans, very fuzzy socks (fuzzy even for fuzzy), and a floppy copper-colored hat made of yarn, hoping to be pinched for not wearing green. She would then either return the pinch with a punch, if pinched by a dork, or with a flirtatious wink and coy giggle if pinched by a cute boy. She plugged in to her iPod and scrolled down to a menu she created of ambient sounds — "elevator" was for riding in elevators, for instance, and consisted of muzak "hits" and uncomfortable silences; "the bus" featured the droning white noise of engines, spinning tires, muffled road rage, and inane chit chat; "dining commons" was a cacophony of plates clanging, mess munching, and the roaring murmur of lunchtime conversations. She opted for "silence" to get her in just the right mood for her murderous — excuse me, express *shippingous* — jaunt to the nursing home and her new vocation as the Grim Reaper's nubile assistant. Reaperette. She turned the volume up high.

♪ ♪ ♪

According to the internet, a violin bow is made of wood and stretched animal hair, typically from a horse's ass — or *tail,* as it is known.   I know of exactly one novel about a violinst, Hermann Hesse's *Gertrude.* The narrator, whatever his name is, is a violinist, fledgling composer, and loner loser who enjoys long quiet walks in the mountains.   Gertrude is the saucy fraulein that he likes. The third character, Heinrich, is a popular opera singer, gregarious lush, and all-around ladies man who takes a shine to the narrator's music — that is, when he isn't shining up the ladies.   They become boon buds and wear lederhosen and yodel and stuff. Herr Narrator loves Gertrude, but Gertrude loves Heinrich.   Gertrude and Heinrich get married. The narrator, whom I will henceforth call Stanley even though I know that isn't right, pines away for Gertrude for approximately one million years, then writes a masterpiece opera for his friend. Heinrich beats the tar out of Gertrude while in a drunken rage — or beats the tar into her, or both — then dies of an exploded hemorrhoid just before the big show. Gertrude

10

has a taxidermist preserve the corpse and she keeps it in the drawing room, oddly enough in a pair of nylon short pants and combat boots. She never re-marries. Driven insane by his own music, Stanley goes postal and assassinates Chancellor Bismarck, escaping into the distant future with the aid of a time machine that looks conspicuously like the Titanic. Well, the first five or six sentences of that summary are somewhat accurate. It is not easy to capture the spirit of Hesse's literary genius in words.

♪ ♪ ♪

Chelsea wasn't thinking of Gertrude as she strolled into the Sunny Pasture Retirement Community, ducking under the dangling green St. Patty's Day streamers. I don't think she has read *Gertrude*, as far as I know, although I would bet she has read some Hesse and probably that blotto buddha jackass Jack Kerouac, patron saint of indolent coffee house hipsters everywhere — and definitely all of the Harry Potter books, since she is a female human in the USA at the turn of the twenty-first century. Right now, however, Chelsea was focused on the plan and that one hundred dollars an hour. There wasn't much to it: (1) smile at the receptionist, (2) offer to play violin for free for the residents, (3) stroll around under the pretense of meeting the old-timers, (3) stealthily squeeze an IV, trip over a cord or two, "adjust" a pillow, (4) be cute some more, and (5) then leave a sparkly flyer at the front desk announcing that a violinist is available for parties, weddings, memorial services (in somber font), and other rites of passage. Ta Da! Bring on the bereaved.

Chelsea handled the whole thing very cleverly, her theater training and natural appeal coming in handy. This is the conversation she had with the receptionist nurse person lady:

"Hi!" Chelsea said cheerfully.

The middle-aged African-American assistant nurse at the desk, Rose, looked up and smiled. "Well, hello! Are you here to see a family member?"

"Uh, no. My name is Chelsea, and I play violin in the college orchestra, and I thought I might volunteer to do a concert or something for the residents sometime."

"Hi Miss Chelsea. That's awfully nice of you. Very nice. Aren't you a sweetie? We do have events like that from time to time, at least once a month. Music is such good medicine. We have a piano in the Rec Room that anyone is welcome to play," Rose said as she pointed toward a large common area down the hall. Chelsea responded by glancing over her shoulder, slowly enough to give Darlene time to anticipate the move and shift positions.

"I have a flyer with my phone number on it, maybe you could post it? I also do, um, family gatherings and things."

Chelsea handed Rose one of the sparkly "too cute for words" flyers, to which Rose gave a cursory but attentive examination and then smiled.

"Why, I'll be happy to. Did you draw this yourself? Isn't that something! What kind of music do you play?"

"Oh, everything! Thanks a bunch!"

"If you'd like, it's visiting hours, and I'm sure the folks would love to meet a cute little young woman like you. You brought your violin with you, I see...."

That was just what Chelsea wanted to hear. "Oh, can I? That would be wonderful!" She then bounced and bounded in signature teenage style away from the desk toward the hallway. Rose stared after her, slightly envious of the girl's warmth, wondering if a fine piece of white meat like Chelsea had ever seen the world, or had a broken heart, or ever really *known* a man. Then she remembered how young she had started, how young everyone starts these days, white, black, yellow, green, or whatever. That was a long time ago, Rose thought, pronouncing the word s l o w l y so that it had several syllables: l-o-o-o-o-o-o-ng.

Chelsea exchanged smiles with quite a few of the elderly residents and carefully surveyed the scene. There were no surveillance cameras in the rooms and most of the more ill patients seemed essentially unconscious. Nap time indeed. In one room Chelsea stood at the doorway, staring for a long time at an octogenarian who slept only a few feet away, marveling at the landscape of her skin, the grooves and dark spots that marked time, the small purple veins on her eyelids, the steady, pained gasp that was her breath. Chelsea moved closer and held her hand near the woman's mouth just to feel what it was like. She wondered, do old people transform into children in their dreams, chasing each other playfully, like dogs chase squirrels in theirs, shaking and twitching their legs, with muffled shrieks and yelps?

chapter three

nero, farza, cleosutra

I would call Chelsea a logical person, certainly in comparison to the average Joe or Joe Bob or Bobbi Joe or Jimmy Clyde Joe Bob Earl. She took a course last semester on logic and rhetoric and got an A-minus. Riding the bus back home after the first killing, immersed in the simplicity and fluidity of what had just happened, the thought occurred to her that the future doesn't really exist—it's just an idea, since when it arrives it is the present and no longer the future. She looked at the clock on her cell phone, 1:47 pm. 1:48, until it hits, is nothing but wishful thinking. It could easily never come at all. Suspense! Now it is an undeniable truth, as everyone will tell you, that children are the future. So, logically, if the future doesn't really exist, that means that children, being equivalent to the future, don't either. And since it is of course impossible to kill something that doesn't exist or isn't real, she could express ship children any old way without committing a real crime, unless the cops also wanted to pin the Easter Bunny kidnapping on her. Man, logic is groovy! Darlene agreed. Q.E.D.

Someone who appreciated the dark side of logic and its immoral potential was the Russian author Fyodor Dostoevsky. Dostoevsky wrote several great novels, including *The Brothers Karamazov*, about three stocky brothers named Larry, Moe and Curly who had all sorts of zany adventures with Cossacks and randy babushkas; *The Idiot,* the tale of an autistic genius played so memorably in the film version by Dustin Hoffman; and *Crime and Punishment,* which isn't relevant to our story here at all so I'll skip it.

♪ ♪ ♪

As the legend has it, the libertine tyrant Nero, Roman Emperor from 54-68 CE, blithely played the fiddle (with his backup group the Imperials) while the city of Rome—a town built almost entirely from wood, hay, dung, and congealed olive oil—burned down around him. We picture flames throughout the city, visible through the palace archways, the huddled masses melting like human s'mores. One problem with this quasi-historical account, Chelsea learned in her World History class, is that the fiddle hadn't been invented yet and wouldn't for at least another hundred years. I doubt that Nero would have successfully built a time aqueduct to go slightly into the future to bring back an instrument in his own time period to learn and then play during the conflagration, but who knows. A more responsible emperor would have also brought back fire trucks and fire extinguishers and a small army of fire-eating X-Men. I guess that's why Nero is reviled as such an irresponsible tyrant. Maybe "playing the fiddle" was just a metaphor for masturbation then, like "rolling the dough" now or "shaking hands with Mr. Happy"? That would explain it. We shall conclude that Nero is still the first violinist in spirit, however. I'm sure the cavemen beat him to the masturbation thing. Maybe being emperor means never having to jerk off, since there would always be a willing sycophant around to do it for you, or at least a slave or somebody. Those were the days.

♪ ♪ ♪

Chelsea has an imaginary friend, Farza. Farza has never met Darlene but he has heard stories. Chelsea has decided not to tell Farza about this new get rich quick scheme of hers. Frankly, she's not sure how he would take it. Even though they are friends, Chelsea feels like there are definite limits to the relationship and it has never been what one might call close or all that intimate. It might be better to refer to Farza an imaginary acquaintance.

A few days after St. Pat's, with already another funeral concert booked and an invitation to perform at the nursing home, Chelsea was sitting even more prettily than usual, basking in the early Spring sunshine. Farza showed up, though, with some fresh cash of his own, coincidentally enough (from god only knows where), and had an excited bee in his man-bonnet about going to see a fortuneteller. "It would be ever-so-fun!" Farza exclaimed, sounding like Dorothy from *The Wizard of Oz*, which he knew always cracked up Chelsea and made her that much more compliant. Chelsea was bored and Farza persuasive, and so after a quick walk of the fingers through the yellow pages, off they went, to a certain Madame Cleosutra, professional psychic and "Future Counselor."

The Wizard of Oz is a charming dystopian musical tragedy about a golden land suffering from an infestation of wicked witches, heartless robots, brainless farmers, and chubby fag midgets all run amok. A tornado touches down and whisks the main character, Dorothy Dandridge, to Ozfest, where she is forced to perform fellatio on the entire road crew of a rock band called Dokken—a grueling, demeaning, endless task which she thoroughly enjoys. But then she wakes up in the shower wearing nothing but ruby red heels, saddened to realize it was all just a dream, according to the authorities.

Madame Cleosutra (pronounced *Clee-o-suture*) had set up her psychic business in the front parlor of a two-bedroom bungalow in a lower class neighborhood not too far from the train tracks. It was relatively close by, so Chelsea rode her bike, with Farza humorously propped on the front handlebars. This was humorous because he fell off more than once, and you haven't lived until you've seen an imaginary acquaintance skin his elbows on pavement at high speed — or "raising raspberries," as Chelsea's mom would say. Each time Farza fell, Chelsea would stop pedaling, stare up at the heavens and laugh and laugh. Raising raspberries is better than pushing up daisies, of course, so Farza took this all in stride. Generally he was very affable; I'm not sure why Chelsea keeps him at such a distance sometimes. Maybe it is because he is a boy. I'm also not sure what she imagines when she pictures his imaginary boy parts.

Madame Cleosutra's space could be characterized as velvety, with the obligatory gypsy vibe, rich in reds and purples and golds and crystal shit. Most of the exotic trinkets around the room and the baubles that filled Cleosutra's wrists were from Walmart and the tapestries and such from Joanne's fabrics. Cleosutra, also known as Mary Ann Oliva, came from a long line of successful clairvoyants, which of course doesn't mean that she had any genuine extra-sensory powers or any more intuition than Chelsea, Farza, or James K. Polk. She was, however, quite adept at the fine art of reading people and separating them from small amounts of money, which done enough times becomes a fairly good living. Mainly Cleosutra/Mary Ann got by on alimony checks from the three ex-husbands who were the three fathers of her three kids, but there's no shame in that. She had a strong feeling each time she was being mounted by these semi-familiar men, her eyes closed in a vain attempt to forget the sweat and hair (theirs and hers), that she might very well become pregnant — especially when they would ejaculate in her without protection, and so it came to pass at least three out of three thousand times.

The most impressive mystical element of the entire room was undoubtedly Cleosutra's shock of white hair, a lightning bolt streak of white in an otherwise ebony coif. This is what in a dog coat is so memorably called a *blaze*; both shock and blaze are great words for it. Cleosutra's shocking blaze/blazing shock (which first appeared not long after she turned 29, roughly ten years prior to this moment) was so striking and effective in dazzling her customers that she completely eschewed the normal gypsy do-rag. This was one psychic stereotype she managed to avoid, and it was a point of pride for her. Chelsea was very pleased by the whole scene! She was extremely fond of gypsy style—flowing skirts, long, surprising scarves, lush colors that clash, all of it—and instantly liked this curious woman with the head stripe and dark eyes, although she was disappointed and found it a bit rude that Cleosutra did not acknowledge Farza.

Famously, the Bride of Frankenstein also had a shock of white hair, and suffice it to say that the carpet matched the drapes (cf. the Director's Cut). Had Frankenstein's Monster not been so afraid of fire, he would have surely gone down in a blaze of glory.

chapter four

jake, darren, aunt amy

Farza sat in the vestibule while Chelsea had her fortune told. Staring intently into her crystal ball, Cleosutra, as usual, didn't see much of anything except her own blob-like reflection (and still no goddamn winning lotto numbers), but, ever the professional, she curled her eyebrows and made something up anyway. Chelsea waited with genuine hope for a revelation of her exciting future.

"You are in college?" This was somewhere between a statement and a question, one of the signature tricks of the trade.

"That's right," Chelsea answered, captivated by Cleosutra's smoky, vaguely Mediterranean voice.

"You like a boy?"

"Um . . . " Chelsea had a few in mind. "Yes.

"From school, yes? He likes you also, very much."

Chelsea smiled.

"His name begins with . . ."

Chelsea was so tempted to try to finish Cleosutra's sentence, but knew to resist.

"J-?"

Chelsea instantly thought of Jake Manson, a boy in her chemistry class. They were in the same lab and they had had two and a half nice conversations. Cool! But Chelsea, being an intelligent young lady, recognized that "J" — particularly in the golden age of Jakes, Jacks, Jordans, and Justins in which we now live — was a very safe guess. Jake was tall, a psychology major with wavy, chestnut brown hair and green eyes. He never said much in class, which Chelsea liked. He seemed very mature and centered, maybe because he spoke so seldom. After lecture one day she asked him how he did on the exam that had just been returned. In a "socially acceptable designated joke moment" he said something at which they both laughed heartily but in retrospect wasn't all that funny or memorable or smart or really much of anything. What really mattered, Chelsea realized, were the signals that suggested he was truly saying to her, "I have fornicated with you in my mind."

Chelsea had been in love before, maybe, she wasn't sure, during high school with a fellow musician, one of those too cool for words jazz-o wannabes, a double bassist. His name was Darren Culp. She had lost her virginity to Darren in that

23

typically clumsy and not very romantic teenage fashion after the junior prom. Of course, both Darren and Chelsea constantly scoffed at the prom as being a conformist bullshit parade, but went anyway and carefully obeyed all the clichés. There was an unstated agreement for weeks that prom night would be the night that his "helmet pal," as he called it – probably because it seemed to always stand at attention and perhaps due to its not so honorable discharge – would enter her fresh young plum. The metaphors here are as incompatible as Darren and Chelsea were. The sex was over quick, of course, and never got much better over the ensuing months. Chelsea could imagine the bed as a stage, which made the event somewhat exciting, but during awkward love-making (more like mauling) in the back seat of an SUV she kept waiting for Jason Voorhees to appear, hockey mask, knife and all. Senior year, with college applications and other things and Darren's insufferable musical snobbery (Jaco this, Mingus that), they drifted apart. Chelsea cried about the situation more than once, but looked back on those tears now as pathetic and embarrassing, much more than Darren deserved. Like any girl in her first real love relationship – and first sexual relationship – she of course fantasized about marrying him and felt used when the "love" he claimed for her and all the "forevers" were proven to be a sham, little more than the outer manifestation of the inner workings of hormones. The

Cinderella story returned to the ether from which it was born: the true driving force of Darren's affection was not eternal feeling but rather surges of testosterone, muffled moans, and messy squirts of semen. This was *Id*, alas, not *I do*.

Although there were some divinely awesome physical and emotional moments, Chelsea correctly surmised that sex was not "all that," but at best only partially that. In college, at a party early her first semester, only a few months ago, Chelsea had a one night stand (or better said, a one hour stand – or even better said, a half-hour lay down) with a boy. She liked his bright blue eyes, pierced nose, indifferent body language, and his pick-up line: "Hey, want to have sex?" When Chelsea didn't say no right away, he knew he could follow with his second line, "Let's get out of here," to which she nodded assent. They did it quickly in his dorm room while a lava lamp bubbled in the corner. Chelsea lived at home and thus didn't have easy access to such sexploits. She found the soft reddish hair on his abdomen particularly fascinating, as well as his narrow shoulders, and stared up at him, feeling detached, the room slightly spinning because of all the flat keg beer she had consumed. He wore a condom and said she was beautiful in between his grunts and thrusts. After "it" was done, the boy (Kevin? Colin? Kelvin?) peeled off the rubber, kissed her, smiled, and said, "well, I'll see ya around." Lickety and then split. Chelsea again didn't mind his directness, but after this, not yet 19, she decided that, used twice, she was in no rush to be a grown woman. She thought he saw him on campus during finals but wasn't sure. She gave a subtle wave from across the main walkway, which this person returned, whomever it was. Such is the Allegory of Chelsea's little sugar cave.

Chelsea remembered something her Aunt Amy had told her not long after the Darren fade-out, that relationships are what kill the dream of love; after a while the hope of romance and "happily ever after" dissolves and we settle for just whatever is around and calls for the least effort, not Mr. Right but Mr. "Good Enough." Mr. Good Enough is someone to watch a DVD with now and then, who will listen to us complain and pretend to care, provide decent sex, comfortable shelter, yadda yadda yadda: not a partner, not a savior, just someone to fill these slots. "Romeo and Juliet had to die for that love to live. In the real world he would have slept with her best friend and Juliet would have developed OCD and gone into therapy," Amy groused. Chelsea's Mom overheard this and called Amy a depressing cynic. Amy retorted, "Look, I'm a forty five year-old out of shape divorced Mom with a dead end job I can't stand, I get chronic headaches, have an irritable bowel, and I think I might be diabetic. I've stayed up past 11 pm exactly five times in the last year. The last guy I dated wears a John Deere hat, and not because he is a Hollywood star incognito. There was no ironic cool in this wardrobe choice, Ellen, just tobacco juice and cow cookies. That I'm still alive and haven't driven my car into the produce section of a crowded supermarket proves I am an optimist. Zippity freakin' doo dah! Go bake a cake and leave us alone." Chelsea liked Amy.

Cleosutra's next psychic bombshell returned Chelsea from her little trip to the past. "You like music?"

Chelsea smiled and nodded warmly.

"And not just to listen . . ." — a dramatic, searching pause — "but to play?"

"Yes, I play in the orchestra. Violin."

And so this dull dance went for the better part of a half-hour. Cleosutra informed Chelsea that she would be a successful musician who would find love in college, have a generally happy marriage, three bright children, would travel late in life, whoop dee doo. Chelsea fully appreciated almost immediately the emptiness and banality of the predictions and couldn't help but feel disappointed.

Most significantly, there had been no mention at all of the express shipping, nothing about Farza, no reference to Darlene. Cleosutra gave her a pleasant hug goodbye and Chelsea complimented her hair. "I knew you would say that," Cleosutra joked, a line now used for the 768th time. Chelsea didn't know this yet, but there was one person in town with legitimate ESP—Ebola Joe, the homeless Vietnam Vet who could often be found in the alley next to the 7-11. Ebola Joe was very much aware of this, though. More on the local yokel oracle later.

Chelsea headed toward the door to find that Farza had nodded off. She nudged him twice in the arm, more like a push, and his eyes opened as his head bobbed from side to side. "All done? How'd it go? Will you marry Brad Pitt?"

"It was fine. She hit the mark with one or two things. Your turn."

"Nah, not me, girl. I'd rather not know my destiny. I'll just wing it through life and act like I know what I'm doing."

"Yeah, why change now. Let's get out of here."

Farza and Chelsea left Madame Cloesutra's Velvety Future Emporium, not any closer to each other than before, with still so much left unsaid.

chapter five

manny, grandpa, noah

Like most people, Chelsea didn't believe in fortune telling. First of all, being able to see the future entails that in some sense this future has already happened, and that certain gifted individuals in the present — "seers" — have the ability to peer into (or perhaps pee into) this other temporal dimension that hasn't occurred yet here but somehow exists somewhere, enough that it can be observed in a crystal (plastic) orb or deck of cards, etc. Secondly, the inescapable implication is that everything is preordained and out of our control. We may go through the motions thinking we have free will, but that only meshes with the "logic" of fortune telling if the results of those supposedly free choices can be known ahead of time. In other words, those choices have already been made at some cosmic level. But if they have already been made and the results are there in "cosmos town" or the "cosmos channel," fixed enough so that they to be observed, how are they choices? Chelsea didn't understand this. Kant, one of the many bachelor philosophers (see Kierkegaard, Nietzsche, Schopenhauer, and basically all the rest), as incomprehensible as he is, basically cut through all this "fate versus free will" bullshit. He spoke of freedom as "a necessary postulate of practical reason," meaning that as a metaphysical assertion it was non-verifiable and non-falsifiable (just like we can't empirically or logically prove there is a God or boogey man with a musket who comes out to hunt in our rooms at night, despite all the drugs we might take, we can't prove or disprove that there is no such thing as Fate). But, Kant insisted, we have no choice but to act as if there is such a thing as free will, as if our decisions are free and fully consequential. (Little did Kant know that he was destined since the beginning of time to think this!) "Practical Reason" refers to both the practicalities of life and the necessities of successful society, as perceived by the rational/moral mind (for him those were one and the same, but he was a bit of an uncompassionate hardass). Freedom is never absolute, since there are limitations posed by physical laws and the actions of others. Chelsea couldn't just decide to dunk a basketball or eat a cruise liner and be able to do it, and as charming as she could be, she couldn't by her will alone make any of us able do it either. Chelsea thought about the ins and outs of freedom now and then, but mostly at her college marveled at how much America's youth took full advantage of the freedom to conform, and how even the non-conformists all did the same non-conformist things.

The fate/free will debate is some age-old doodoo, that desiccated white kind, no doubt. However, the ultimate philosophical question to thinkers like Kant, of course, is "Why can't I get laid? Should I read more books?" Kant eventually died when the time-zeppelin he was piloting crashed into the Super Bowl. It was a good death. As it spiraled in fat turns, nose-first, plummeting towards the stadium, Kant ("Manny" to his friends) had two nagging, screaming thoughts amid the terror: *are my papers in order? and if they are not, will anyone notice?* God laughed so hard at this that it rained shit.

While exasperated by philosophy, Chelsea has always been very interested in the paranormal, much more so than the normal. She read a biography of a Bengali yogi who could levitate and supposedly didn't eat food for twelve years. Apparently air and the Hindu equivalent of the Holy Spirit were enough to sustain him. When Chelsea was still in grade school she sat in the library one week and read nothing but Time/Life "Mysteries of the Unknown" books. There was one on UFOs, another on Stonehenge, the Pyramids, the Elephant Man, and Elvis/Jesus. Her favorite favorite *favorite* thing, though, is films

31

about zombies, such as *Dawn of the Dead*, *Shaun of the Dead*, and *Anne of Green Gables*. But she wonders why zombies, so desperate to eat brains, never try to eat each other's brains. Otherwise so wild, they seem to draw the line at their own kind and have this weird sense of mutual understanding, even solidarity. Zombie commies! She asked Farza about this one day and he said that zombie aficionados like her need to "get a life," which might be true but didn't answer the goddamn question.

Definition: Philosophers are those who eat their own brains? Their own rectums? Hmm . . . Either way, the department of philosophy swimsuit competition at Chelsea's college would not be something to watch.

♪ ♪ ♪

One thing Chelsea does not tolerate is intolerance, especially racism, although personally she had not known too many non-Caucasians in the various communities in which she had lived in the inland Northwest during her short lifetime. In college she was learning to hate all white men (the heart of the core curriculum these days), which really isn't that difficult, so her first semester grade point average was high. She was glad that she and Farza (of Persian descent) had chosen an "ethnic" fortuneteller to visit. Chelsea's late grandfather was a hardcore racist. He used to pepper his morning conversation with remarks like "an apple a day keeps the niggers away" and had similar n-word variations of all the major familiar aphorisms: "A penny saved is one a nigger doesn't have," etc., etc. Grandpa even offered this take on the old Zen Buddhist koan, when he once asked Chelsea and her mother: "If a tree falls on a nigger in the forest, does anyone care?" She and her cousins were watching a basketball game, and he walked in and inquired, "Who is winning, our niggers or their niggers?" One day at Dennys with the whole family, Chelsea's grandfather refused to be served by a black waitress, or "goddamn nigger" as he called the young lady to her face. It was quite a scene. Chelsea hid under the table. Occasionally he also referred to African-Americans as "kaboonies." When her grandfather was wasting away, dying, his body gnarled and contorted, when he barely could recall her name or even his own, did he still remember his racist hate? Thinking back on this shameful part of her family heritage, Chelsea resolved to make sure that her exploits at the retirement homes would be race-blind. Equal opportunity expresss shipping! Or, better yet, maybe she would get rid of the honkies first. Darlene did not object.

Christian racists like Chelsea's grandfather often cite the Curse of Ham as support. The story involves our old friend

33

Noah of the boat party. As is described in the Book of Genesis, Canaan, son of Ham and grandson of Noah, was chillin' in Noah's tent one evening, when Noah entered in drunk and naked or partially naked, sliding across the floor *a la* Tom Cruise in *Risky Business*. Singing karaoke, Noah did not notice young Canaan at first, and Noah's wang may have been hanging out (Biblical scholars differ on this). Canaan, understandably, laughed and pointed. An embarrassed and enraged Noah then cursed the boy, his father, and all their descendents (the Canaanites) to be enslaved for this heinous act. Later whites, with their well-known penis envy, would see this curse as a Biblical justification for the slavery and maltreatment of Africans. Since Noah was one of God's favorites, it was like it was straight from the Big Cosmic Honky himself. The result: American history. Isn't religion awesome?

chapter six

wolfgang, god

For the next funeral service, Chelsea was asked to play a mournful rendition of "Ave Maria," the Mozart classic. The Academy-Award winning film *Amadeus* gives us an inside look at the life of Wolfgang A. Mozart, particularly his raucous college years and time as a fraternity pledge. After the fraternity is placed on "double secret probation," Wolfie and his brothers decide to throw a killer toga party. During a performance of "Shammalammadingdong" by Otis Day and the Knights, the frat house is attacked by a swarm of Nazi locusts riding great white sharks in a tsunami of blood. Mozart is one of the few to survive the carnage. Ave Maria was written for his date that evening, Maria, the 15-year old Mozart deflowers. When he discovers that she is the daughter of his bitter rival Dean Salieri, hilarity ensues. In Latin "ave" is a salutation roughly translated as "hey, nice rack" or, in southern Italy, "shake it, shake it, shake it!"

Mozart, like Chelsea, was a young violin virtuoso. Chelsea took up music out of a sincere longing to create beauty, a conscious drive even at the tender age of six, and she perceived beauty most clearly when she listened to music. After her mother steadfastly refused to buy her a vibraphone, despite Chelsea's little girl tears—"I'm sorry, honey, they're just too expensive," and so on—the two settled on a violin. Chelsea's fingers and soul found a comforting haven in the instrument immediately, and beauty flowed from the union soon after. Mozart, in contrast, took up music because his upwardly-mobile father, who saw it as a good way to gain favor with the Hapsburgs, rather forcefully insisted and beat the living piss out of little Wolfgang on a daily and nightly basis.

Chelsea's father died when she was only four years old. He contracted a debilitating liver disease and rapidly wasted away at age 40. She doesn't remember much about her Dad: just hazy, nebulous images apart from one solid memory of him lifting her near the ceiling fan and tickling her one morning, and his booming voice that spurred on her frantic giggles. Since he died, Chelsea's mother would date local losers now and again or the occasional "genuine prospect." These relationships or futile attempts at relationships never lasted long. She and Chelsea didn't talk much about it. One night Chelsea woke up after a disturbing dream and went to get a glass of water and an aspirin; she found her mother crying to herself at the kitchen table, eating strawberry preserves straight out of the jar with a serving spoon. Their eyes met in a surreal, frozen moment — it was as if her mother were a deer in the headlights. And as if the driver of the car were a deer also.

"Oh, hi honey," her mother said, wiping her eyes with the side of her hand and fighting back a sob.

"Hi. Are you okay? Can I get you some bread . . . or, uh, insulin?" This broke the tension and her mother laughed. She swallowed the last vocalizations of her deep pain, pushing them far down inside again, stood up and hugged her daughter tightly. Chelsea closed her eyes and could feel her mother's heart beating. That embrace continues.

♪ ♪ ♪

The popular sweetener *honey* is secreted from the glistening buttocks of bees (*Apis mellifera*) who have engorged themselves on pollen, a sticky, addictive substance that is nature's heroin. Wild honeybees were first domesticated in Mesopotamia four thousand years ago by trapping them under empty yogurt containers. Bee wranglers, as they prefer to be called, would then corral them with tiny lassos woven from silk and the delicate eyelashes of oxen. This gave way to the much more efficient "bee beard" by the late first millennium BCE.

Human beings (*homo sapiens sapiens*, literally "smarty smarty pants"), meanwhile, are still undergoing the process of domestication. They are kept in cages with shredded newspapers, junk mail, and empty beer cans, run on wheels for exercise, and secrete books—or more often, dance music. Humans, with a degree of intelligence unsurpassed in the animal or vegetable kingdom, are the only species in nature that occasionally choke to death from the improper chewing and swallowing of food, and also the only species known to refer to themselves in such a clinical fashion.

♪ ♪ ♪

Early during the second week of the express shipping, God visited Chelsea. This was a first. He took the form of a glowing pile of dirty laundry in her room.

"Chelsea."

"Yes?"

"Chelsea. Talk to me."

"Is this God?"

"Yes."

"Well, I'll be da- . . . darned." Pause.

"What are you doing, my child?"

"Oh, you mean the . . . you know."

"Yes. Why have you chosen this path, my child? Is it for the music or the money?"

"In the grand scheme of things, Lord, I think they are both the same, don't you? Isn't everything one?"

God pondered this for a long time, while the laundry continued to glow, brightening and dimming as if breathing, a pulse created by God's thoughts.

"I like money, Chelsea. Send me some."

"Will do. What kind of cut do you want?"

Chelsea and God then haggled as if it were a Middle Eastern market and reached a mutually acceptable dollar amount.

chapter seven

hate

Things Chelsea hates, in no particular order:

•The stickers on fruit, CDs, and DVDs, and the sticker shrapnel they leave behind that has to be scraped off with a fingernail or vigorously rubbed off over hot water. The stickers that are impossible to cleanly remove from new non-stick frying pans are particularly ironic and cruel.

•The gluey smudge left behind from the previous.

•Farts in the shower, the smelly kind that cut right through the steam.

•Fundraising pledge week on PBS, especially when it is called "Festival!" or something deceitfully celebratory, and those gushing shills who keep begging for money and won't let us get back the show.

•Stoplights that turn yellow and red immediately after being green, so that maybe one car and a half get can through — if they hightail it. It's like someone is intentionally trying to drive everyone crazy. Maybe the guy whose job it is to monitor the cameras at intersections is amusing himself by being a fucking asshole.

•When her eye twitches. There seems to be no pattern or rule to it—it doesn't seem to matter whether she is tired or not, anxious, hungry, whatever. It just does it sometimes.

•Houses painted yellow. There is a house in her neighborhood that used to be a giant white cube. Now it is canary yellow. When Chelsea first saw it, she thought it was a colossal tidal wave of piss about to crash down on her. She still ducks and cowers when she can't avoid walking by it.

•The sensation of her teeth skidding along the skin of a peach. Ewww. She would rather go through the Chinese water torture.

•Loud inane conversations between the bus driver and passengers about gas prices, the weather, vacations, vaccinations, anything. Isn't there a law against that? She wonders this every time, then plugs herself into her iPod.

• People who say, "There oughta be a law." There should be a law against *that*.

• Audible, obnoxious, persistent tongue-clicking. If this were the felony it should be, Chelsea's Mom—an inveterate tongue-clicker—would be in the slammer or possibly forced to wear a scarlet "T".

• The smell of roses and rose milk perfume. Once she ate rose ice cream in a Persian market (Farza's idea) and thought she was going to barf.

• People who insist on categorizing and labeling others. Chelsea derisively categorizes such people as "Labelers." Whenever she hears someone doing this—such as on the bus at loud volume—she angrily mutters under her breath, "damn Labeler!"

• Those who have no empathy. Chelsea just can't understand what's going through the minds of people like this.

• The Velcro strap on her right sandal that keeps coming loose. And the fuzz and such that gets trapped in the Velcro buds rendering them non-clingy.

•The use of "disconnect" as a noun, as in "there is a disconnect here between the policy and the practice." What's next, "a separate," "a confuse"? At what point did "disconnection" stop being a word? Why do people even bother to speak if they are just going to say stupid shit?

•People who blast music from their bedrooms or living rooms when they take a shower, as if they need a soundtrack to scrub their butts or are preparing for a title-fight. Can they even hear the music in the shower? Or is it for their dramatic towel-wearing return to the room?

•Fingerprint smudge on clear tape — like when she is wrapping a present or a package and handling tape, trying to get a nice clear spotless piece, but her fingertips keep leaving marks. Wearing gloves doesn't help, since they leave fuzz, and she is not going to buy unfuzzy gloves just to be able to use invisible tape. One solution she came up with recently was to put tape on her fingertips. She liked the feel of it and kept the tape on for the rest of the day. Her mother saw this and said, "I'm not even going to ask." It seemed like taped fingers and/or unfuzzy gloves might also minimize computer keyboard grease build-up, which she also hates.

chapter eight

norman bates

Oh detritus! Oh damp! Just around the corner from where Chelsea and her Mom live is a recently abandoned motel, the Paradise Creek Inn. Chelsea used to call it the Purgatory Reek Inn, hardy har har. It was a dreary beige stucco eyesore before and a disaster after, as it awaits demolition. Some windows remain, others have been replaced with cardboard or clear plastic tarp. Signs and bright yellow tape warn intrepid trespassers that they will be prosecuted. Walking alongside the temporary metal fence that guards the parking lot, Chelsea finds the whole thing creepy, especially the small mountains that have formed on the pavement of discarded bad art, detached doors, and the jagged chunks of particle-board furniture, smashed from being tossed over the balcony. And there's always something unsettling about an over-stuffed dumpster. She is particularly depressed by the mattresses left out to get rain-soaked and mildewed, thinking of the poor families who could have used those. This motel taunts the workers of the world with its ritzy and chintzy garbage, she thought (she was learning about Karl Marx in school). According to her mom, the site will be the future home of yet another chain drug store, Sav-on or Rite Aid or Walgreen's or CVS or Sav-Rite or whatever. Goddamn the pusher man. Chelsea stared at the yellow big cat tyrannosaurus rex demolishing the second floor and wished she could saddle up this beast and tear down a different motel, the one where she and Darren spent the night after the prom. Later she checked on the web and learned that this type of heavy machinery is known as an "Excavator." Others include the bulldozer, crane, and cranedozer. Light machinery would be something like an electric can opener or salad shooter.

The most famous motel film, *Psycho,* is a macabre gem by the obese limey master of suspense, Alfred Hitchcock, about a cross-dressing serial killer whose father in the end is revealed to be Darth Vader. Darth Vader, when not nourished by the "dark side," would feed on crackers and rolled-up cold cuts that would be inserted through the grates on his helmet, washed down with juice boxes he would drink through a straw. His diet was understandably limited. In a poignant scene, Vader advises Norman to use Liquid Plummr on a nasty hair and blood clog in one of the motel showers. Father and son embrace while the latter nervously adjusts his silk panties. Vader, meanwhile, wore black metallic boxer shorts that needed no adjustment. Such is the force. The two laugh after the Vader's headgear accidentally cuts Norman above his monobrow.

Another Hitchcock classic is *The Birds*, in which debutante Tippi Hedren is attacked by swarms of flying rabid piranha hot for her Chanel suit and white gloves. The birds symbolize birds.

Chelsea hasn't stayed at too many motels in her life, maybe a dozen during family trips or for music events that called for traveling, but she enjoys looking at herself — and occasionally touching herself — in motel mirrors, the noisy tumbling sound of ice machines, shiny white bathrooms with toilets that have been sanitized and sealed with that paper strip, and continental breakfasts, except for the room temperature milk.

chapter nine

the orchestra

Chelsea tries to practice the violin at least an hour every day, in addition to the times when the university orchestra assembles. The young conductor, Stefan, a new faculty member in the music school, is a bit smarmy, not the most approachable soul but nice enough, although probably too much of a perfectionist. He tries to offset the vulnerability of his youthfulness with excessive formality. Chelsea recognized right away that he didn't have the same emotional connection to the music or love of beauty that she did, but she likes the pieces he has chosen for their spring concert, especially Dvorák; she generally loves Sibelius but not so much the particular symphony chosen. As the seventh violinist in the large ensemble, Chelsea usually feels like just a cog in a machine. She doesn't know too many of the names of her fellow musicians and doesn't care, although the boy who plays the glockenspiel is cute. The first bassoonist usually has crusty boogers in his nose. The second bassoonist is a blonde girl with a bob haircut; she has such tiny fingers, like a cupie doll's. Chelsea wanted to see how far she could bend them back. The harpist seems like a bitch. There is a female tubist, rare in this world, who has lungs like a whale's and could start at nose tackle for the football team. The percussion section probably has circle jerks (except the glockenspieler, she hoped), including that weird girl who plays the snare. Chelsea loves the sound of the oboe, not just the instrument but the word itself. Listening to a sauntering oboe solo to her was like dreaming while awake, and worth all of the work and BS of playing in the orchestra. Apart from moments like these, she was thoroughly disillusioned with the whole enterprise.

Emile Durkheim, the French sociologist, wrote of "collective effervescence," the transcendent, bubbly feeling one gets when part of a large group acting in unison, one voice in a heavenly choir. Alka seltzer is an "effervescent medicine." It goes *plop plop fizz fizz.* To Durkheim, this fizz was not only the essence of religion as a social institution but the very substance of religious experience itself. What we mistake as God (plop) is in truth just our awareness of the power of the collective (fizz), in those moments when it becomes one force so much greater than the sum of its individual coordinated parts. To Chelsea it was a sexual feeling—the sounds of the orchestra sweeping up from underneath her, the music embracing her from all sides, lifting her up. She felt it in her loins, her womanhood. Chelsea wondered if the other violinists, most of whom were playing the same exact phrases as her in a coordinated movement that would be beautiful even with the sound turned off, were enjoying this orgy going on. *Oh what a relief it is.* Did the conductor know he was directing an elaborate porno?

This summer the orchestra has a series of concerts planned in St. Petersburg, Russia, as part of an international Rachmaninoff tribute connected to the famous Stars of White Nights Festival. It will be Chelsea's first trip out of the country, only her third time on a plane (not including once in a helicopter), and she is excited. St. Petersburg was built out of muck and swampland single-handedly by the Tsar Peter the Great, who was eleven feet tall and flossed his teeth with railroad ties. He wanted Russia to be more Westernized—and to have a lookout point to keep track of those mischievous Finns—and Moscow was too far East, a town of thatched huts, igloos, defecating bears, and bearded women. St. Petersburg's modern wide streets were rationally arranged based on the latest Enlightenment-era ideas, paved with beets, golden potatoes, and imported coconuts.

Most of Chelsea's violin teachers when she was growing

up were dry taskmasters, experts primarily in vicarious power trips and psychological abuse. Only her love for the instrument carried her though these tedious hours. There was one notable exception, Mr. Cellini, a near-sighted, middle-age manic-depressive widower with unusually fleshy earlobes, an avuncular disposition and unctuous skin ("avuncular" and "unctuous" being two words Chelsea remembered from her Word-a-Day calendar). Topping this off was a stringy comb-over that was far from flattering, but Mr. Cellini also had the most beautiful hands and was strangely sexy. His playing was so tender and lyrical. There was truly music in his soul that Chelsea could hear and wanted to know.

Mao Tse-tung proved that a balding man with a greasy, stringy combover can nonetheless be viewed as an infallible god by approximately 1 billion people.

chapter ten

carrie and jerry

Although not many of her orchestra mates are among them, Chelsea has real friends, of course, as much as any of us do. One girl in her English class qualifies, Carrie, also a first year student. Chelsea and Carrie shared a mutual dislike of their English instructor (whom Carrie referred to as "that bloodless toothpick cunt"); Chelsea thought Carrie's tongue and eyebrow piercings were cool, as was her jet-black dyed hair and raccoon make-up. It was a very rare look for this part of the world. She was less enamored with Carrie's tendency to say forced hip things like "Right on" instead of "yes" or "yeah," not to mention her cigarette smoking. Carrie was much more of a confidante than Farza. For instance, Chelsea told Carrie about her "one hour stand" not long after it happened. Carrie said "Right on, good for you," but then warned her to be careful.

"Let's just say I've had a few and have gotten a few gifts that have kept on giving."

"What do you mean? Stalkers?"

"Oh yeah, some of that, too," Carrie said with a smirk, taking a drag from her cigarette. "No, I mean STDs."

"Really?"

"Oh yeah. No picnic." Whatever doesn't kill me and isn't syphilis makes me stronger, said Nietzsche. "Did he wear a condom?" Carrie asked.

"Uh-huh."

"You sure?"

"Of course, I saw it."

"Right on. Good. And you had a boyfriend before?"

"Yeah, Darren, in high school."

"And you did it?"

"Uh-huh, not that much."

"Did you two use protection?"

"Most of the time."

"Hmm. Well, good, I guess . . . although I guess I should take my own advice. My boyfriend now, or whatever he is, it isn't always so safe. Goddamn asshole."

"Carrie . . . have you ever been with an older boy?"

"You mean, a man, ha. Sure. Guess how old?"

"25?"

"Older."

"30?"

"Getting there!"

"Wow. 35? 40?"

"Bingo."

"What was it like?"

Carrie paused to think. She was only a few months older than Chelsea, maybe a year, if that, but to Chelsea it could have been eons. Carrie tapped the ashes from her cigarette into an empty water bottle. "I don't know, different. More serious. Efficient or something."

Chelsea pictured a teacher with dignified salt and pepper hair passionately kissing her friend's neck, with shelves and shelves of well-worn copies of classic literature in the background, but the reality was probably more white trashy.

Carrie interrupted that thought. "Yeah. I think if I didn't spend half of high school balling I could have gotten into a better college, maybe Ivy League or Berkeley. Ah, innocence lost."

"What do you want to do after?"

"I don't know, be an artist or actress or something. Get out of this dink town, either way. I already can't fucking wait. My theater class is cool, though. I like it. If I could play violin like you things might be clearer."

"I don't know either. It's hard to be a professional musician, from everything I've heard. It's so competitive. I love music because it makes me feel so . . . free, you know . . . but it isn't really like that in orchestra."

"Right on. But there's so many other forums for music."

"True." Perched on Chelsea's shoulder, Darlene giggled.

"Just got to shine, I guess," Carrie said. "You and me both. Make mud pies, sculpt the crap into something beautiful. 'Found art' and all that, know what I mean? Or whatever. Want to go get some coffee?"

"Okay. I don't have class until 3."

"Right on. I'm giving myself the rest of the day off, well-earned, if I say so."

The conversation moved to the Café. It was still a bit cold to sit outside, so the coeds found a spot indoors by the side windows, warmed by the sunlight. Carrie asked Chelsea about her religious views.

"I guess I'm spiritual," Chelsea said, staring down at the table and nervously spinning a sugar packet with her fingers. "My Mom was religious I know, when she was younger, but then something happened."

"Maybe she read a book."

"Ha."

"What does she do for a living?"

"She is a receptionist in an office. Sales, typical business environment, that whole world, you know."

"Hmm. Being around salesmen could kill a person's faith."

"I think it had something to do with my father. I don't know."

"You and her don't talk much?"

"No, not really."

"Wow. I tell my Mom everything."

"Everything?"

"Almost everything, sure."

"She didn't freak out about your tongue or your tattoos?"

"This?" Carrie stuck out her tongue and wagged her piercing, as she loved to do. "Nah, she was a bit of a hellcat when she was younger, the '70s and all that."

"So she's not religious then?"

"Mom? God no! I mean, aside from doing yoga and putting up Christmas trees and the meaningless stuff that everybody does."

"Do you think there is a higher power?"

"Hmm. A tough one. I don't know if it matters, Chels. I mean, think about it, God tells you to love your neighbor, right, and you have to make a leap of faith to love the guy, but so many people get lost along the way and just end up hating and even killing. History is a religious bloodbath. It seems like it would be easier just to make a straight jump toward people. Cut out the middle man. Loving is always a leap, so it's just a straighter route."

This made sense to Chelsea. "Do you think God speaks to us?"

"What, directly? Well, I've never heard him. And he doesn't seem to do much about all the evils in the world. You'd think He'd watch the news and do something. It's on all damn day. Everything bad is just a test of faith? I don't buy it. Nope, no way. Does God speak to you?"

"I had a dream the other night where He talked to me."

"God? Oh yeah? What did He say?"

"I don't remember all of it, but I think He said to send money."

Carrie paused and then exploded in laughter. "Right on! Good one. You had me going for a second! You've got that sneaky sense of humor. Ha!" The customers at the next table stared over at Carrie, clearly eavesdropping and clearly offended; she gave them a very dirty look in return and told them to "get bent." She then did an about face and looked over to the bookish-looking young man with thick glasses seated on the opposite side. "Do you have a problem?"

"N-no."

Carrie noticed he was scribbling away in a sketchbook, hundreds of small smiley faces, clearly a symptom of graphomania, an early sign of schizophrenia and other serious mental illnesses. "What are you drawing anyway?"

He pushed his glasses up his nose with his index finger. "I like smileys. They are the happy place I wish I had. . . . I like the way they seem to mock me with their grins."

Carrie reflected on this and thought of the perfect response: "Right on." Chelsea wondered if everyone in the world, in some way, like Mr. Smiley here, is not just weird but utterly insane.

On campus, when the weather gets warm, the more devout Christian students gather on the mall to strum acoustic guitar and sing folksy gospel songs, closing their eyes and standing in a circle, swaying back and forth with the music while tenderly praising Jesus. Both Carrie and Chelsea find this not just annoying but nauseating and think it should be a jailable offense. Carrie often screams at them at the top of her lungs, "First Amendment! First Amendment!" or "Learn the goddamn blues!" or, best of all, "Virgins!!!" Chelsea can't help but to crack up but also, at least at first, she would tell Carrie that this was rude. Carrie dismissed it with a raised hand. "Ah, they need sinners to save. Gives them a sense of purpose and identity.

They take comfort in knowing they aren't me — but that if they are good little Bible-thumping evangelical angels, spreading the word, singing that divine crap, I could be them, and should be, yay salvation! I have seen the light, Chelsea! It is very white and suburban, wearing a sweater, playing guitar poorly!"

One afternoon, one member of the grassy knoll Christian singing circle decided to return some of Carrie's abuse, yelling "Witch!" Carrie then took off after the girl, who at first sought sanctuary behind the guitarist but then decided it was best to run down the hill as quickly as possible. Carrie chased her for a good half-mile, throwing clumps of mulch at the fleeing soprano, calling after her in sick delight with a devilish impression of Edward G. Robinson from *The Ten Commandments*, "Where's your messiah now?"

Giving up the pursuit, Carrie made it back up the hill, short of breath. With her hands on her knees, coughing and panting, she confided to Chelsea, "Man, I gotta quit smoking if I'm going to run down these Jesus freaks."

Chelsea admired her fearless, blasphemous, over-sexed, goth-ish friend. No wonder Farza had such a crush on Carrie. She did have one serious character flaw, however, as Chelsea and Farza both agreed, which was her tendency to have a bottle of spring water with her wherever she went, and she was constantly sipping. This was even more offensive than the cigarettes.

"Does anyone need that much water?" Farza asked one day. "I mean, she's hyper-hydrated. It's like a baby carrying around a bottle. Is she planning on crossing the Sahara or something?"

"With that and the cigarettes, I think she has an oral fixation."

"Ooh, I bet you're right — good news for me!"

"That's disgusting, Farza."

"I didn't invent oral sex, Chelsea."

"But you would have invented it if you had the chance!"

Farza scratched his chin. "Well . . . that's true." Farza knew when he was licked.

♪ ♪ ♪

Someone else who used to say "right on" was the hippie patriarch, Jerry Garcia, the iconic guitarist and singer for the Grateful Dead. In 1995 "Jerry," as he was known to his adoring fans, a heavy drug user, died from an exploded gall bladder and complications related to advanced body odor. He then ascended directly to heaven on a shaft of psychedelic light, where he now can be found eating ice cream with his fat hands and shooting up.

Carrie, however, took more style cues from punk rockers like John Lydon of the Sex Pistols, a.k.a. Johnny Rotten. Lydon is best known as the co-host of the very successful morning talk show of the 1990s, "Regis and Kathie Lee and Johnny Rotten," and for his charming profanity-laced weather reports: "Oy! There's fuckin' rain comin', you bloody corporate gits! Wankers!"

chapter eleven

jenny, sierra, and lance

Chelsea knew well enough to pace herself, to space out the express shipping exploits at several different nursing homes and to choose her victims carefully — only the most elderly and infirm, so as to not arouse undue suspicion. One afternoon she found herself at the nursing home she would come to call "Shady Quakers," her pun on the standard "Shady Acres." She gave it this name because of the long, dark hallway and general pall of death that hung over the facility during afternoon naptime; the cranky receptionist happened to be wearing a sweatshirt with "Philadelphia" stitched on it, the kind purchased by tourists, hence the Quaker reference. The one exception to this dour scene was a bright sun-filled room with a nice old woman named Jenny. Jenny, although frail, was quite lucid and she and Chelsea had a very warm conversation that day, after

Chelsea poked her head in to measure up the inhabitant as a potential parcel. She was surprised to find a set of alert eyes greeting her.

"Well, hello, aren't you a little angel!"

"Hi! I'm Chelsea."

"Good afternoon to you, Chelsea. My name is Jenny."

Chelsea moved closer to the bed.

"Come, come, Chelsea my dear, sit down."

Chelsea took a seat next to the bed, noticing the slightly itchy feel of the wool afghan draped over the back of the chair.

"What brings you to our happy dreary home?"

"Oh, just visiting. I thought I would come to offer to play violin." Chelsea raised her violin case a bit so Jenny could see it clearly.

"Aha, you play violin? So that's not a tommy gun in there. Isn't that wonderful! Are you in orchestra?"

"Yes, at the college."

"I used to play piano myself, before ol' Arthur got to my fingers."

"Arthur?"

"Arthritis, hee-hee." Jenny showed Chelsea her twisted hands. "No picnic."

"Wow." Chelsea moved in close to get a better look.

"You can touch them if you want, they won't break."

"Are you sure?"

Just as Chelsea reached toward Jenny's fingers, Jenny darted her hand out and quickly snatched Chelsea's arm. The young girl was deeply startled and let out a gasp.

"Got ya! Got ya with the claw!" Jenny had a bright, musical, melodious laugh like birdsong. Chelsea couldn't help but laugh. Jenny sat up straighter in the bed, wiggling herself into place.

"Let me tell you, Chelsea, my dear, it's no joy-ride getting old. These hands are just a small part of it. Diabetes, osteoporosis, gallstones, bladderstones, on and on."

"Do you have a family?"

"I have a son who lives in town not far from here, but he travels so much for work that when I got real sick he had to put me here. Two grandchildren, one in Iraq with the Air Force . . ." she paused to turn a framed photograph toward Chelsea," "Michael, he is a Sergeant, and another, Josh, away at college back East. You look like just about Josh's age."

"I'm nineteen."

"In school?"

"My first year."

"That's nice. So many girls get led astray beforehand. And you want to be a musician?"

"I think so."

63

"There aren't too many things in the world more fulfilling than music. My son could have been a pianist. He was good. So much talent!" She closed her eyes for a few seconds, swimming in some distant memory.

"What happened?"

"He was more interested in sports and things, then his father died when he was only 13, and he didn't care about much about anything at all. So now he is basically a salesman. He's good at his job; I don't think he hates it, but I think I'd prefer it if he did."

"Only one son?"

"My husband and I tried a few times, we wanted a girl, then came the accident. Car wreck." She paused, then pointed to a photo of her husband on the night table in a dark gray suit. "Such a handsome man."

"My father died when I was young."

"Such a shame." Jenny's voice became quiet, hardly a whisper. "Such a shame." Chelsea stared down at her own hands and didn't speak.

"I tell you, Chelsea, I never thought I'd be a grandmother. Certain girls you meet, it's like they're born to be grannies," Jenny continued, brightening up. "They usually have names like Clara or Zelda or Olive or Dolly or Dot or Lottie. Grannies or flappers, fated from the moment they're christened.

I thought I'd skate by with a name like mine!"

"Jenny is a nice name."

"Do you think it's grandmother material?"

"Hmm . . . I think so. It might be borderline. I think it may be defined more by the baking of cookies than by the name."

"Ha! Cute girl! Are your grandparents still alive?"

"Just my nana, my mother's father."

"And what's her name?"

"Louise."

"Hmm . . . definitely a nana. 'Chelsea,' that one I don't know. Maybe," she added pensively.

"I like your blouse."

Jenny was wearing a silk or rayon top with what seemed to be small little smiling jellyfish crossed with flowers.

"Ah!" She looked down at her arm and touched the material. "Yes, the scrubbing bubbles!"

"Scrubbing Bubbles?"

"You ever see that ad with the cartoon scrubbing bubbles?" Chelsea gave her a clueless look. "No? I'm so old. They kind of looked like this. They'd march around and scrub your sink, get rid of the rings, you know, the gunk." Chelsea giggled.

The clock on the wall struck the hour. Two.

"Well, it's time for my story! Would you like to stay here and watch with me?" Jenny reached for the remote and now had a zigzagged thumb poised to press the power button.

"Sure. Story?"

"Oh, soap opera, that's what us ol' timers call them. Do you watch?"

"Not really. Which one is this?"

"Another World. Can't claim it's false advertising! It isn't sci fi but it sure isn't this world." The two shared another laugh.

Chelsea snuggled herself on the chair, tucking her knees under chin and wrapping her arms around her legs. Jenny briefed Chelsea on the main characters, who was currently banging whom and who banged who in the past, and Chelsea ascertained that basically everyone and their evil twin had nailed everyone else in the cast at some point. Some sort of kidnapping was getting everyone's attention now, a comely lass named Sierra with impressive artificial boobies whose father Lance was a millionaire jet-setting playboy oil magnate, now faced with a sudden non-tanning related crisis—it appears that he was finally learning family values.

"He never paid that girl any attention at all, and now look at him," Jenny pointed out.

"Do you think he will pay the ransom?'

"Those kidnappers are tough customers. The detective wants to do some kind of set up, but I wouldn't play games with those guys, no no."

There was the obligatory scene where police officers attempt to trace the call from the kidnappers, while urging the desperate parent to extend the conversation, but then there isn't enough time.

"Christ Almighty," Jenny said with real consternation, her arms folded on her chest. "I've been watching TV for seventy years and I don't think I've ever seen a call get traced. How long does it take?"

"Hee-hee. Or they could use star-69. And wouldn't the central phone company computers know where the call came from?"

"Ha, now you're thinking. But then they wouldn't be able to drag this thing out for a month."

"And not as many commercial breaks."

"Right, right, it's a conspiracy! Where's that nurse's button! Get me the White House!"

Again, Jenny and Chelsea enjoyed each other's humor. Leaving that day, around sunset, after having hugged Jenny goodbye and promising to visit again soon, Chelsea felt pangs of guilt about the killings. For the first time she really allowed it to enter her brain as *killings*. What if she had taken someone like

Jenny early? Could she kill a person Jenny or her own nana? Had she already? One thing was certain: she'd have to find some younger, less appealing people to kill if she was going to keep up this game . . . er, business. She felt a strong compulsion to go home and play violin and forget about it all.

chapter twelve

death and the maiden

Chelsea went home to her room and popped in a recording of *Der Tod und das Mädchen,* or, as it is commonly known in English, "Death and the Maiden," Schubert's string quartet no. 14 in D Minor, D. 810.   It was one of the more interesting titles in classical music, with two things not usually associated at all, unless one considers the *petit morte* or "little death" that the French call the orgasm. At first Chelsea planned to play along, but she set down her violin, turned off the lights, closed her eyes, and just tried to imagine the story Schubert sought to convey with this music.

The first movement, the Allegro, is dramatic, sharp, sneaky in parts, with car chase elements — driving, insistent phrases, abrupt stops, frantic repetitions that have a trance-like effect on the hearer and the performers as the maiden herself is drawn into the back alleys of her destiny and the serpentine twists of fate. The instruments themselves seem to collectively implore, "What has happened here?" Some of it sounds like a prance through flowers, but then something clearly happens: Music comes in and out of the shadows, it stabs and jabs, there is violence — a death — and yet still a very girly, youthful quality. The piece seems to start just after the deed. We as listeners are in the girl's frame of mind as she stands before this body. Her lover? Her tormenter? The gentler parts feel like recollections. Or perhaps there is this doomed romance, with subtle hints of the tragedy to come, the reaper lurking in the yard, a wife gradually learning of the betrayal and slowly slipping into murderous insanity. In all of this, the cello is not as prominent as it should be, Chelsea thinks. It needs to underscore the darkness. Schubert has made it all sound too light, too much like a sewing mishap. Or maybe it's just this arrangement, the recording.

The second movement, Andante con Moto, has tempo and spacing that suggest Mozart's requiem. It is mournful, somber, beautiful, yet, unlike the requiem, has a hopeful quality, a turning. Chelsea can hear tears falling softly but also restraint; she can see the wings of doves fluttering, a restless child's confused, furtive glances, looking to the gathered adults for an explanation. Chelsea can picture her round cheeks and dirty blonde hair. The cortege moves slowly, as if the wagon hearse is floating and dissolving in a mist. The clouds gather, and it begins to rain, then faster; tentacles wrap around the mourners, they are joined in some way by the crime, by pain, these weaving, intricate lines. Roughly halfway through the movement there is a sudden aggressive part, a loud and almost shrill call followed by gentler response, but each comes to more and more be one. Who is calling? Who has responded? It sounds as if the maiden has been confronted, is being scolded, shaken. The pace increases, suggesting evidence being hurriedly concealed. Then it settles down again, a meadow scene and soft interiors; no one is losing sleep. Or is it the peace of the unknowing? But aren't we all complicit? As the second movement concluded with its slight sinister return, Chelsea could see the faces of all those she had helped die, their eyes frozen open, the connection that binds us all. What have I done? What have I done? But then no time to reflect, only run.

The third movement, Scherzo (Allegro Molto), starts up-tempo, with piercing lines, then it begins to drift. There are interesting violin parts, but this movement is boring, Chelsea thinks. It doesn't add much of anything. Here Chelsea pictures the musicians more than any scene of the possible story: the players weaving back and forth in their seats, leaning toward each other and then back as they emphasize and punctuate their respective parts. The third movement goes fast and feels like filler.

The fourth movement is entitled "Presto," as in *Abra-Cadaver*. The opening sequence evokes a galloping horse or horses and recalls the music used when the gates are opened at Churchill Downs, that classic horse-racing theme everyone knows when they hear it, or at baseball stadiums before the crowd chants "Charge!" Could it be yet another chase scene? Chelsea wonders. It's like a trite action film that won't end. When will they catch the bitch? It doesn't sound like brooding cosmic forces in pursuit, which would be interesting, just plain ol' people. Wearing hats, she thinks . . . and at night, except for the maiden with her tousled locks flowing wild behind her. She can hear that vividly. A moonlight hunt. This movement is very self-repetitive, with only slight changes, but the subtle variations do create suspense. What it needs, Chelsea recognizes in a flash of insight, is more death and less maiden. She can hear the little darting slippered footsteps of the maiden; Schubert's message must be that the maiden cannot shake death, and he intended to juxtapose the cheery youthfulness of certain of the melodies and the brisk tempo with the looming, encroaching sense of death, to heighten the tension. But the tone is wrong, the pathos not quite right—it sounds more like she is trying to get gum out of her hair. The flourish at the end is tame. Has the maiden been taken, captured, abducted, seized?   Yes, but the surprisingly undramatic final notes suggest that there is more to be told — in other words, a crummy sequel. Chelsea decides to call death by a proper name: Harold.

chapter thirteen

skippy

After all these memorial performances, Chelsea could trace in her head the pattern of wallpaper on the wall of the funeral home; standing off by herself, she reached out and touched the paisley gold relief, dreamily following the swirls with her fingertips. This contemplative moment of oneness of mind with space and texture was soon interrupted. From over her shoulder she heard a familiar raspy voice:

"Why hello, Chelsea."

As if stating some cruel, repulsive, inexorable truth of the cosmos, she responded dryly, "Hello, Gerald."

"I guess we've been double-booked!" Gerald punctuated this comment with his trademark snorty, uncontrollable, always inappropriate geek laugh. She wondered if he would need his inhaler. It turns out they both had been scheduled to perform for this service, one after the other, which was news to Chelsea.

"Boy, business has really been something lately, huh, Chelsea? I can barely keep up with the gigs! Betsy can barely handle it." *Betsy* was the name he had given to his accordion, a blight upon all girls and livestock named betsy forever. More chortles. After he had gotten a grip on himself, he asked her, "Have you been playing much? Funerals, I mean."

"Yes, two or three a week."

"Wow, I've had almost as many. I wonder why." Gerald wasn't sharp enough to be implying anything.

"I don't know. It must be the flu going around. You know how it is when it hits those nursing homes."

"True. Maybe it's ebola! Eee-bola!" Snort snort snort. This was not funny.

"What song are you playing today?"

"'Our Lady of Spain.' Mendez family. An accordion classic. And you?"

"The Tennessee Waltz."

"Now that's an interesting combo! I wonder what be third in that series. It's kind of a math problem. Spain, Tennessee . . . "

Chelsea wasn't so mature as a college student to not ever want to play along, and there was humor in this line of speculation. And Gerald's awkward small talk and semi-flirting was slightly more tolerable than the endless parade of old folks telling her how pretty she was, asking her if she was in school, etc. "Well, geographically, maybe 'Blue Hawaii'?"

"Ha! Good one, Chelsea! Blue Hawaii! Elvis!"

Some of the mourners were starting to glance over angrily at the overly-jocular teen. The funeral director stood in the corner frowning, motioning over to Chelsea to get Gerald's attention.

"Whoops, Gerald," she said just above a whisper. "I think Mr. Connors wants to see you."

Chelsea watched Gerald's sunny expression instantly change to one of genuine fear. Gerald, basically afraid of all authority figures and far too dependent on these funds for his comic book collection, turned slowly away from Chelsea and shuffled over slowly to be reamed and excoriated by the grim funeral director, who then led him away to the main office for a assertive reminder of funeral home etiquette and his "final warning." Hopefully Connors was also telling him to wash that greasy hair.

"Hey Chelsea." This time the voice was Darlene's. Chelsea tried to ignore her.

"Chelsea, you know we have to do something about him."

"Why? He might be getting fired as we speak."

"No, I doubt it. He'll send a few tears down his pimply cheeks and be back on Connors' good side. He's probably gumming the ol' guy's cock."

"Darlene!"

"What? You know how it is. Just a fact of life. If he liked girls he probably would have asked you. Might still anyway."

"Gross. Please leave me alone."

"Did you hear what the dork said? He's asking *way* too many questions. I think he is on to us."

"Gerald? No way. He still hasn't figured out how to tuck his shirt into his pants instead of his underwear."

"Maybe he likes it that way. Have you tried it? I think he's smarter than he lets on."

"No, I think he is much, much dumber."

"He's taking our gigs, too. We're doing all the work, taking all the risk. How much money have we made so far?"

"I don't know, maybe $1500?"

"Damn, we'd have almost twice that much if it weren't for him."

"So?"

"You know what."

"What? Get rid of him? Won't that be just a bit

suspicious?"

"Hmm." Darlene sat down at the edge of Chelsea's neck, the very image of Rodin's thinker. Then the proverbial light bulb appeared over her head. "Got it! We should find out if he has any allergies. A guy like that I would bet has all kinds of allergies. Accidents do happen."

Chelsea was forced to share a meal with Gerald and a few others one afternoon. This did ring a bell.

"Nuts."

"Are you giving up already? C'mon, Chelsea!"

"No, nuts as in nuts. I think he is allergic to peanuts."

"Peanuts! That's fantastic! But how many would be enough to kill him?"

"Or maybe all we need is just enough to knock him out of commission?"

Darlene glared at Chelsea as if she couldn't believe what she was hearing. "Please. Better safe than sorry. The world will be much better off without him, trust me. You know that. The odds are slim, but it is possible he might reproduce someday."

Chelsea had to concede this point. "Yeah, you're right. He has to go."

The wheels were again turning. Soon a few proposed plans were in the works, being mulled over by the girl and her shoulder devil. One intriguing idea was of the poison peanut butter kiss, *a la* Mata Hari meets Skippy, but this would involve a full lip-to-lip encounter with Gerald; this was not an option unless Gerald magically turned into George Clooney. Chelsea had no interest in getting that close to Gerald's zit farm and Darlene preferred to not have that image seared into her little brain. The problem, clearly, was how to get that much peanut butter or the requisite number of cashews into Gerald's system without him realizing it and without having to get too close to his skin or B.O., and in a way that it couldn't be linked directly to Chelsea. Preferably she wouldn't be anywhere near the scene or, if so, could pass for just another inconspicuous face in a crowd. She could sneak nuts into his snack plate at one of these little memorial buffets, concealed in his ambrosia salad or something, painted white to blend in with the marshmallows — or grounded into a fine dust that could sprinkled into almost anything. Another option would be to drug him by slipping over-the-counter sleeping pills in his drink (Chelsea's Mom had bottles of these in the medicine cabinet of her bathroom) and then fill his mouth with peanut butter cups, pushing the first few down. A nerd with a mouthful of chocolate wouldn't arouse suspicion. But they'd need privacy, the opportunity might not come. And his parents would wonder why he would suddenly forget his allergy. The peanut dust was a better bet. Still, Chelsea had a humorous vision of surreptitiously attempting to chuck peanuts from across the room into Gerald's open mouth while he snored . . . and pecans wedged in each of his nostrils. She couldn't help but laugh out loud. An ancient mourner with bluish silver hair seated not far away shushed her; Chelsea apologized sincerely, grabbed her violin, and went into the other room to tune and get into the right frame of mind for the Tennessee Waltz. It was the next day that Chelsea started carrying a Ziploc bag of ground peanuts with her in her purse to every occasion, just so that she wouldn't forget.

♪ ♪ ♪

Tennessee, nicknamed "The Nougat State," was the 16th state to join the union, in 1796, just after Hawaii, and was the 11th and last to declare that it was bolting and seceding at the beginning of the Civil War. Tennessee has a long history of hesitating before finally making the poorest possible decision. Tennessee is home to more than four universities, two major airports, and approximately 8,350 caves, all centers for advanced waltzing. Franklin Delano Roosevelt, during the New Deal, established the Tennessee Valley Authority (TVA) to bring hydroelectric power to Tennessee's numerous moonshine distillers and pig-fuckers. 87% of that hydroelectricity is used today to power neon Budweiser signs throughout the state. The best-known version of Johann Strauss's Tennessee Waltz was recorded by Patti Page in 1950; Jerry Lee Lewis married his first teenage bride with the song playing in the background. The city of Nashville is known for its scale replica of the Parthenon of Athens, made entirely out of nougat and platinum blonde human hair, hence the state nickname and state color.

chapter fourteen

po boy

This has to be the most boring class in the world, taught by the most boring professor. Chelsea envies the deaf. Who thought history could be so meaningless? Whose idea was it to let the dead lecture about the dead? Didn't Jesus say something about that? Will anyone resuscitate the past? Today's pointless lecture is on the social structure of the Middle Ages, blah blah serfs and the lords' turf, feudalism who freakin' cares. The "teacher," in his infinitely uncharismatic manner, has managed to make this about as entertaining as watching road crews paint a highway. Chelsea wants to scream: give us some of that sexy self-mutilation they were into, the bubonic plague, something on the Crusades, show us *Monty Python!* As the instructor droned on, Chelsea's eyes became heavier and heavier, her head sagged . . .

"Chelsea! Chelsea!!!" She suddenly heard her mother's

voice, a persistent knocking on the door, she awoke to find herself in her bed at home. The entire classroom scene had been a dream, she realized. Chelsea was relieved at such an easy escape from purgatory, but was disappointed that her dreams had become so mundane and dull. Apart from that, she had a hilarious case of bedhead.

Chelsea unlocked the door and peeked her face out, yawning: "Mom?"

"Honey, there's a man here to see you."

"What time is it?"

"4:30 or so. You fell asleep after school."

"Oh . . ."

"Come on out, he's in the living room."

Chelsea staggered to the other side of the house, still very groggy. Seated by himself in the middle of the drooping couch was a 20-something year old man in a suit, probably 28 or so, medium-height, a bit portly, but otherwise very handsome. He stood up and introduced himself to Chelsea, handed her a card, mumbling something about wanting a sandwich. She thought he said that he was a police detective. Perhaps the jig was up. No jig lasts forever, not even Lord Shiva's. Chelsea felt slightly terrified and wondered where she might have slipped up. There must have been some DNA, there's always the DNA.

"Excuse me, did you say you wanted me to get you a

sandwich, officer?"

"Officer? No, I'm sorry. No, I just said that my name is Mr. Stepanovich, I'm a legal aide, a paralegal and investigator, the assistant to the attorney that handles the estate of Jenny Andrews. The card . . . "

Chelsea read the card, and sure enough that's what it said, Porfiry Stepanovich, legal attaché, clerk, etc., for the firm of McKinnon & Hanson.

"A mouthful, I know. It's Russian. You can call me Po, everybody does. I'm here on business, but it is just a matter of clarification."

He had a sweet smile, she thought. "Andrews?"

"Yes, apparently you met Mrs. Andrews last week at the Shady Acres Retirement Home."

Oh, *Jenny*, she thought. "Is she ok?"

"Oh, fine, fine . . . or rather I should say the same. But the reason I'm here is that . . . um, Mrs. Andrews amended her will last week to include you, and given the circumstances, it is standard procedure for us to confirm that this is a legitimate change. Her son is a bit concerned."

"Me?"

"I can't go into the details of the adjustment, but it is true you've been added to the will. May I . . . ?" He pointed back to the sofa, asking to sit. Chelsea nodded and sat down next to

84

him, at a safe distance, as he took out a small notebook and began jotting notes, talking as he went, glancing up occasionally, pausing slightly whenever his eyes met Chelsea's. She was, after all, an attractive young girl, and he was very single.

"Such changes like these are not unusual, but certain elderly individuals, women in particular, as they get near the, um, end, sometimes make erratic adjustments in their estate, leaving thousands of dollars to animals, for some reason usually cats, or disreputable organizations . . . "

"Like religions?"

"Right, ha . . . " He scored points with her for recognizing the joke here and laughing, however uncomfortably. Po did not have an easy manner, as they say, and felt there were important expectations of formality with his role. ". . . Or fraudulent charities, so we have to check it out."

"I understand, I think."

"Can you tell me about the circumstances in which the two of you met?"

"Well, it's nothing really—I play violin at retirement homes and hospices now and then, and I just happened to meet Jenny one afternoon . . . Tuesday, I guess. We talked for a while, watched television."

"You talked for how long would you say?"

"Oh, all together, I'd say an hour or so, maybe a little

85

more."

He was writing much more now than what she just said, she noticed.   "Uh-huh. And I can ask about, uh, what topics? Just generally speaking."

"Well, generally speaking, I'd say family, mostly. Her husband died young, my father . . . my father died young also."

"I'm sorry."

"That's ok. It was mostly about that, and the soap opera we were watching together."

"Soap Opera?"

"Yeah, *Another World*, I think."

"Ah. Got it." He wrote the name of the show in his book and underlined it and put it in quotation marks. "Was Mrs. Andrews . . . how shall I put this . . . did you see her take any medication during this time you were in her room?"

"N-no, I don't think so." Chelsea wondered about this question. "Can I ask why?"

"Oh..." Porfiry cleared his throat.   He hated "interrogating" such an obviously innocent girl. Or, he corrected himself, *young woman*. He could imagine himself with her, but then again, he imagined himself with almost any woman he encountered, at least for the possible "geometry" of the sex. He could vaguely remember sex; it had been more than a year, and kind of a disaster the last time. He previous "lover," a law student that he had met through a friend, wore too much make-up for his taste and seemingly had slept with half of the U.S. Marine Corps, and apparently wanted the sex to be more like pummeling or perhaps an invasion of Afghanistan. Her single redeeming feature, apart from the basic T & A, was a mole just about her left breast. Po would still probably give the world to kiss that mole once more. Maybe it was waiting for him in hell. After the woman coldly dumped him, he wrote a note to himself, about himself, and put it on his refrigerator: *What is a Fool?*

"I'm sorry," he continued. "We need to ascertain Mrs. Andrews' state of mind during your meeting, to assure the family that she was of sound mind, etc. No offense." His tone was sincerely apologetic.

Chelsea didn't know what to say. "She seemed very clear-headed to me, I guess. I have nothing to compare it with, though, since that was the first time we spoke, but compared to most people I talk to, not just old people, she seems more than fine."

"Hm. She is in the early stages of Alzheimer's, you know."

"Really?"

"Yes. It comes and goes, though, from what I understand. Sometimes she is perfectly lucid, other times not.

87

You must have caught her on a good day."

"That's terrible."

Porfiry forgot his notes for a second and his voice took on a vacant but also more sincere quality. "It is awful. My grandfather had Alzheimer's. I watched this proud strong man become so helpless. It's hard to describe . . . it's like a slow tearing away of the self from the self. A long, involuntary suicide. The worst kind of torture, where your loved ones become strangers right before your eyes. I wouldn't wish it on anyone."

Chelsea sat in silence. What a beautiful man, she thought.

"I should apologize," he said as he closed his notebook and put his pen in the inside pocket of his suit, and stood up to leave. "Anyway, I think this is all fine. I can see why Mrs. Andrews was so impressed with you." They both blushed. Just then Chelsea's mother entered the room with a tray of tea and the teapot reserved for the most special of guests.

"Please sit down, Mr. Stepanovich, won't you stay for tea?"

"Oh, I shouldn't."

"No, no, sit, please. There's always time for business, not always time for good company." This was one of Chelsea's mother's favorite sayings, and she was exhibiting the maternal instinct of flirting for her daughter's sake. "Did Chelsea mention that she is in the college orchestra . . . and single?"

"Mom!"

"What? It's true, isn't it?" Full as ever with nothing but good intentions, the older woman was quite skilled at playing innocent.

Porfiry smiled and chuckled along with Chelsea's self-satisfied mother. Chelsea was embarrassed but also thought *please mom don't stop.*

♪ ♪ ♪

Tea came into this country along with the British during colonial times. The new white "Americans," drawn from the homeland by the desire to practice their slight variations of Christianity and have human slaves in peace, shared in the imperial addiction to the hot caffeinated brown-water delight. During the nineteenth century, Great Britain fought two wars in China and forced the Chinese to become opium junkies so that it might continue to have a steady supply of inexpensive tea (the triangular trade route with India that some of us learned in high school history class). Several decades before that, the tea-addicted founding fathers of the American Revolution — better described as pouty teenagers — decided, when the British raised the tax on tea, to go to war rather than pay. Disguised as Indians, a group of sneaky colonials, in act of wanton mischief and the kind of destruction of property that we call terrorism when other people do it, trespassed onto one of His Majesty's ships in Boston Harbor and chucked crates of tea into the drink.

chapter fifteen

shitheads

It was a pleasant conversation. Chelsea managed to indiscreetly tamp down her bedhead and could feel herself being charming, even coyly seductive. Chelsea's mother was very interested in Po's law school experience and, of course, broached the girlfriend subject. Now that everyone knew that everyone was single, Chelsea thought, true communication — and true lying — could really begin.

"We have a regular Lonely Hearts Club meeting, don't we, Mrs. Walker?" Po joked.

"Yes! Please, call me Ellen. I feel old enough as it is."

"Ellen."

"Would you like to stay for dinner, Po?" Given the tone of the banter thus far, this was a well-mannered, natural suggestion, seeming only slightly forward.

"Oh, I'd love to, I would, but I really can't. I need to get back to the office. My boss has a trial that starts tomorrow and I'll be up most of the night getting everything ready."

"Are you sure? That's a shame. Are your parents in town?"

"No, they live in Boston. I came out to Seattle for law school and somehow found my way out here. I like it most of time, and even when I don't, it still feels like home, if you know what I mean."

"Hmm . . . yes, I do. Do you believe in chance with things like that, or fate?" Chelsea's Mom could get philosophical now and then, often inspired by folding laundry and other repetitive household chores. ("Sisyphus should try this," she once said.)

"That actually is something I think about now and then—every little thing that had to happen just so for me to be sitting here right now, drinking this particular kind of tea, having this exact conversation with the two of you."

"Which would you prefer, chance or fate?" Chelsea inquired, sensing the answer might be very revealing.

"I don't think I'd want to know either way. If it's fate, um, I don't know, I'd have to say, at least at this point in my life, it's a . . . "

"A let-down?"

"Chelsea!" Her mother exclaimed. "That's not polite."

"No," Porfiry continued in an encouraging tone, "that's just the kind of phrase I was looking for. You have to wonder about those of us who have . . . um, *small* fates. And if it's chance, it's just too crazy and senseless. And then I think, maybe there's some awful fate just around the corner, then fate would . . . "

"Suck." Chelsea said. Po's eyes met hers and this was definitely a *moment*.

"Or maybe there's something amazing waiting for me, for all of us, but it's a million miles away, what are we doing in the meantime. . . . and then what are we, just puppets or pawns, or more important pieces on the chessboard?"

Ellen chimed in. "When I was still in the church, the idea was that God has this master plan, yet we have free will, the freedom to sin or not to—but he knows all of our choices beforehand, so he can be all-powerful and at the same time . . . "

"Not responsible for any of the bad stuff that we do," Po interrupted. "I learned that, too. It never quite made sense to me."

"Did you grow up religious?"

"Not very. My family is Russian Orthodox."

"Such beautiful churches!"

"True."

"At some point I decided to keep Chelsea away from

93

religion, or at least let her make her own decisions. I think she turned out all right." The mother gave the daughter a look filled with real pride, accompanied by an awkward squeeze.

"So is this now the Lonely Hearts Atheist Club? Or do you talk this way to all the Jehovah's Witnesses, Mormons, salesmen, and repairmen that come by?" Po said out loud, for the first time showing his more cynical side.

"Repairmen of the spirit! I think we both believe in God, right honey?" She glanced at her daughter then back at Po. "But I feel like with all the religions there are, especially the Middle Eastern ones that have dominated the last two thousand years, that something's wrong."

"Like they got the wrong guy." Chelsea added, smirking.

Po was starting to deeply enjoy this line of dialogue but was at the same time feeling self-conscious, like he was a character speaking in a novel rather than a real person. "I know what you mean. Sometimes, though, I wonder if, um, you know, if there's some self-centered error in thinking that God must prefer people like us, who are more free-thinking, humorous, educated, lonely, etc. I mean, why should whomever or whatever He or she is love Liberals or the tolerant or swing-dancers . . ."

"I love swing-dancing!" Chelsea interrupted, to which

Po responded with a smile, met by another admiring look in her eyes, before collecting his thoughts and continuing.

"If God is a free being, the ultimate free being, who knows what he loves or wants. Maybe he loves . . . "

"The shitheads!" All were surprised when Chelsea's Mom said this, even her, and both Po and Chelsea exploded in laughter.

"And boogers!" Chelsea said.

"Air pollution and pop tarts!" Po added. Suddenly it was an iconoclastic giggle fit. "Maybe He doesn't love this kind of fun irreverence at all."

Chelsea couldn't bear such a terrible thought. "Ah, I hope He does."

"Anyway, kids, enough of this small talk! I think our handsome guest needs to go, and don't you need to practice, Chelsea?"

As Po was leaving, he asked Chelsea for her e-mail address and a phone number where he could contact her in case he needed to confirm some of the information from today — which was a very real possibility and not just a sly way of potentially inviting her out on a date. Walking back to his car, his mind was buzzing, his heart felt alive again: *wow, she is very cute, and her personality is perfect. Fate indeed! It'd be cool to be with a girl who isn't so experienced and cynical and used up. This could be the one.* Then he reminded himself that the "One" thinking is always trouble, a self-made trap in the making. *And will I corrupt her? Am I just attracted to her innocence?* And God chuckled. Po had just about given up on "real women," and maybe this budding attraction to a college fresh-woman was another symptom of that. Ten years is a long time. But Po couldn't help himself. He felt good, a sensation of joy only slightly tempered by dread of the hurt that could come if he should let himself love again. *When I'm 120, she'll be 110.*

♪ ♪ ♪

As Chelsea's mother closed the door, she said to her daughter, "What a nice young man. I think he likes you."

"Do you think so?"

"Mothers know these things."

"You certainly made it painfully obvious that I was available!"

"I'm sorry, honey. Better me doing it than you, right?"

"I guess."

"Life is too short for games. I wasted so much time playing games with boys and driving them crazy when I was young, keeping them confused and guessing just because I thought that was what good girls were supposed to do. I wish almost any of them were with me now."

"Do you really think he likes me?" Chelsea asked again, hopefully.

"Yes, I certainly do. Anyone could tell. And you looked so beautiful. How could he resist? My darling girl. You knocked him dead." Ellen held her daughter's hand and kissed her forehead. *Interesting choice of words,* Chelsea said to herself.

The human mind generally works by associations. One of the great moments in the history of thought occurred when caveman Og made the logical leap of more or less equating *this* (a.k.a. thing 1) to *that* (thing 2), classifying, grouping, counting, likening, etc. This is the beginning of both mathematics and poetry. Continuing this tradition, Chelsea decided that Po had a Jimmy Stewart quality in his appearance and demeanor, albeit compressed. In one of his more beloved roles, as Elwood P. Dowd in 1950's *Harvey*, Stewart played an alcoholic gadabout prone to hallucinations — maybe — whose best friend was apparently a 6'5" giant cross-dressing rabbit: that is, a male rabbit who would dress as a female marmoset. Chelsea watched this DVD with Farza, which they both enjoyed even though the notion of an imaginary rabbit friend was preposterous.

chapter sixteen

yo einstein and omygod jack

Chelsea was so distracted by the Po possibility that she almost forgot that she needed to express-ship Gerald. (She was tempted to use the phrase "rub out," but that caused her to imagine Gerald "rubbing one out," i.e., masturbating, which made her shudder. But, she had to acknowledge, Gerald did it, likely several times a day; she did it occasionally; probably every other human being including Jesus and the Buddha did it, and the birds and the bees, if they can't, would do it if they could. Hmm, she wondered, how many non-human species wack off? Or is it *whack*? Whack on? If you whack off too much do you find yourself out of whack? And why does "whack job" have an entirely different meaning, as in "She's crazy, a whack job"? And was jacking off named after some overly self-indulgent dude named Jack who got caught spanking it or something, so that he became synonymous with onanism in his tribe? And how is it that with intercourse we get off by getting it on? Language sure is funny when it comes to sex, she thought.) Fortunately, Darlene was on top of things: "Hey sister, while all this is making me very horny, try to remember the geek," she whispered. "Get your peanut act together! Time is money."

Cliché Logic: If money is the root of all evil, and time is money, then it follows that time is the root of all evil. Hard to argue with that. Apart from aging, erosion, entropy, it's just the backdrop where everything has to happen. As Einstein showed, also, as part of his theory of general relativity, time and space are inseparable. So space, therefore, is money and the co-root of evil. Evil thus has to take root in time and space, which made perfect sense. And money is relative. Chelsea wondered where light and energy fit in with all this, if it is impossible to travel faster than the speed of money, but she's no physicist and so went to crush some nuts.

♪ ♪ ♪

That night, when Chelsea lay down to sleep, she said in the darkness, just audibly, to no one but herself, "I love you, Po." She probably didn't mean it, but with love and landmines I say close enough.

Po worked late at the office, until after 3 a.m. When he finally made it home for a catnap, before spinning right around and going back in to work, he was so exhausted he had forgotten to take off his shoes. His last thought before drifting off was of Chelsea. "I love you, Chelsea," he testified in his solitude, the night blue with early morning light, the horizon glowing. He meant it, but was it his limited sense of Chelsea, the idea of her, a simulacra, or was it really *her*? It didn't matter.

♪ ♪ ♪

The excavators and excredozers have been working overtime lately, and now the motel around the corner has been completely razed to the ground, all the junk removed from the site, the pavement and concrete ripped up and transformed into mud. The very definition of progress. The crews seem to be digging a new foundation for the drug emporium. On the morning after Po's visit, they had turned off the water in the neighborhood, apparently in order to have most of it flow down the street. Chelsea slept in and her mother had left for work; she found out about the situation when she heard the toilet shaking, the pipes rumbling like a Harley with the throttle open — or more aptly said, a Harley being driven by a yak and pecked by geese and flying lawn mowers. Fearing it might be the worst possible thing to do, she couldn't help but flush. The water that streamed down was mud-brown, almost black. *Gross, I hope that's topsoil and not poop water.* She went outside and over to the site in her fuzzy bear slippers to ask what was going on, raising the question to the first construction worker she found.

"Yeah, sorry miss, the water will be on and off for the next few hours while we get this all ready to go. Don't use it for a while."

Nice of them to tell any of us. Chelsea waded through the rising, ankle-deep water back to the house. Perhaps the new plan was to have the drugstore be lakefront property, ha. Louis XV, King of France and Emperor of Luxembourg, haughtily stated *Après moi le Deluge*—interpreted as "after me comes the flood," illustrating supposedly his vainglorious lack of concern for the future, or his sense that France (and Luxembourg) would soon be up shit's creek without him. In essence, it has been supposed, his proclamation was "I am the be all and end all," or, to put it in early 1990s ghetto slang, "I am the *shiznit*," or yet again, "you motherfuckers can all get stuffed." For this he has been unfairly vilified. In truth, ol' Louis was really just incontinent, with a leaky bladder to go with his cleft palate and over-used poop chute; he had quite a different flood in mind.

Chelsea went back inside, grabbed an apple ("red delicious") from the counter and sat down to check her e-mail,

101

hoping for a letter from Po. The psychologist and philosopher William James spoke of death as the "worm at the core," always in there eating its way through any juicy happiness that we think might actually last. Goddamn worms. As she logged in, she saw three new messages, not counting the spam, one from Carrie about the English homework, one from her orchestra conductor about the spring concert, and one from her mother informing her that the water might be shut off; in the last one, in typical maternal overkill, her mother also said that she would was also sending her a text message about the same in case she didn't read the e-mail. *Sigh, no Po.* Did she misread the signs? Chelsea started to reply to Carrie when — presto! — a new letter instantly arrived from PorfiryS@mckinnonhanson.com! Chelsea beamed, caught her breath, crossed her fingers, and excitedly opened the letter. This is what she read:

> *Dear Chelsea,*
>
> *If it is not too much trouble, I'll need to meet with you, preferably today or tomorrow to confirm some of the information we discussed yesterday concerning Mrs. Andrews. This is standard procedure in cases like this one, but I want you to know that I think you are quite remarkable and you've left a very strong impression on me. (Off the record, I have every intention of asking you out to dinner sometime.) Tell*

your mother thank you for such a surprisingly
wonderful conversation yesterday. I look forward to
seeing you again.

Yours truly,
Po

Po was aware that he had taken a big chance in writing this, one that could theoretically cost him his job. He wasn't always the sharpest knife in the drawer, but he did know when a girl liked him, and recent events had convinced him that life is far too short to let opportunities like this pass by, despite the undeniable conflict of interest with his role for the law firm. *Ethics schmethics.* And fuck this job; he wasn't so enamored with the law anyway, or kissing his boss's ass with the hope of someday having his own lackeys to order around. *I'm smart, I work hard, people like me (I think). I'll go do something else if I have to. With her.*

Chelsea knew from how he wrote "Po" at the bottom and not "Porfiry Stepanovich, clerk" that this was more than just a friendly invite. And this was no ordinary "yours truly." Yay! She felt butterflies and some other flying insects buzzing in her stomach and electricity in her toes.

Although she wasn't a game player, Chelsea was familiar enough with "the rules" to know she shouldn't respond right away. She'd try to wait at least two hours or so. Meeting today was probably out of the question anyway, since the prospects of a shower were slim, thanks to the drug store construction crew.

With the time to kill, she surfed the web a bit, checked out cnn.com and the news on the latest natural disaster *du jour*. It occurred to her that Cleosutra had said nothing about Porfiry or the inheritance, both fairly significant cosmic events to say the least. She realized she hadn't even thought about Jake, the boy she liked from school, for days. There was only one course of action: the Magic Eight-Ball.

Popular during the 1960s and 1970s, the Magic Eight-Ball was an over-sized replica of an eight ball (as in billiards), filled with some sort of gelatinous psychic juice and floating triangular answers to yes or no questions. One need only submit an inquiry, shake the ball vigorously, and *voilá,* the gods would give a reply in the form of a blue triangle with white ink that would appear in the viewer — or cleverly postpone a reply, "Ask Again Later," "Outlook Uncertain," etc. Other possible responses include "Yes definitely," "Absolutely," "My sources say no," and "No way!" One flaw in the mechanism is that the same question posed more than once or only slightly altered (later specified as being "against the rules") could yield completely different answers — which was frustrating to say the least. There are now internet versions of the same which have fixed some of the glitches. Chelsea asked the online 8-ball several times whether "Porfiry Stepanovich" loved her, whether "Porfiry" loved her, if "Po" was "the One," and so on. She received a strongly affirmative reply 19 out of 25 times. *Good enough for me!* she concluded. This was true love. No questions about Jake were even necessary.

Since what would have been breakfast had become lunchtime because of her late rising, and because an apple only goes so far, Chelsea went into the kitchen and made herself a sandwich in Po's honor, with roast turkey (she was not yet a vegetarian), mayo, bean sprouts, and pickled cherry peppers. She then went back to the computer to send him a response, as nearly two hours had passed.

> *Dear Po,*
>
> *I enjoyed our time together yesterday also, as did my Mom — I think she might have a crush on you! I can't meet today, since I have to go to church to pray for all of our souls and then broker a Middle East peace settlement, etc., but tomorrow afternoon after Orchestra practice would work. Do you know the concert hall on campus? You can meet me there at 5. (Oh, and off the record and on it, I'd say yes).*

Yours,

Chelsea

Chelsea didn't want to be too forward, presumptive, or easy, but she felt it important to be encouraging and playful: to give him a true sense of her personality and humor, to start things off—if there were to be beautiful, honest things—right. She thought for a long time about every word and phrase, and how to make the note feel spontaneous. The very first clause she typed and erased, typed and erased, but finally decided upon it after she realized that you can't spell together without 'to-get-her,' which suggested a world primarily consisting of just him and her, exactly the impression she wanted to convey. She felt much more comfortable—more *herself*—writing. Maybe he would show up early and see her play violin. If he did, she thought, this would be a very good sign. Since practice often didn't end until 5:15 or so, this was a well-engineered moment in the making. She wondered if she should try to get rid of Gerald today somehow and have that all out of the way, or wait. If she were going to start dating a young professional like Po, she would need money.

Po was thrilled by Chelsea's letter, finding it humorous and charming and altogether impressive, with such a lively voice—although he wondered if her mother really did have a

106

crush on him, and what that sort of "joke" might mean psychologically. Hmm . . . it had been a long time since college and PSYCH 101. The mention of any female being attracted to him was a good thing, he determined, and this was also likely an indication that the mother and daughter had discussed his qualities as a suitor. And it felt liberating to be able to joke around about religion with anyone. *No cross up her ass,* he thought to himself, crudely. 5 pm presented a bit of a dilemma, however. Should he request to leave work early, go home and clean up first, then show up to meet Chelsea, looking overly fresh, or should he just arrive on scene in his usual office attire carrying the possible stink of the day? What should he wear? Should he shave or look semi-grizzled and cool? Should he plan on having dinner with her, or just play it by ear? He laughed to himself, *am I becoming a girl?* Po decided that it was a healthy thing that he felt sort of nervous. All he had to do was explain to his boss that it was a follow-up interview for the Andrews case, maybe offer to make it non-billable, etc. But the trial BS might call for more of his time, he could get pinned. Hmm, better ask the boss now. *Angels don't piss on my head.*

Po phrased his request well, making it sound like a necessary errand; the boss said that it was fine; he was on top of things with the trial and court wouldn't be starting the next day until the afternoon, so Po could have the night off. With no

107

hitches in the plan, Po felt free to respond to Chelsea. It took him some time to think of "casual," humorous response.

> Dear Chelsea,
>
> I will see you at 5 tomorrow. That gives me time to find a solution to global warming, scuba dive to the lost city of Atlantis, and run for President of Argentina.
>
> puppies and fuzzies forever,
> Po

chapter seventeen

sibelius, huck finn, filbert

Chelsea listened to her cell phone messages and lo and behold she learned that she had another funeral gig, for that Sunday, playing right into her plan; she e-mailed Gerald and asked him if he wanted to accompany her, and he eagerly agreed, responding within minutes. First would be a Saturday afternoon rehearsal, and that would mean curtains for the geek. Enjoy your last few days of life, Gerald, she said to herself. Kiss that accordion goodbye.

The next day was an exciting one, as Chelsea happily, anxiously, slid along with time toward her date with Po, with destiny.

The orchestra had just started a run-through of Sibelius' Symphony #4 in A minor, Op. 63, when Po entered, instantly mesmerized by the brooding, elusive music, and his eyes found Chelsea. She noticed him and gave him a conspiratorial smile. He quietly sat in one of the plush auditorium seats.

The first movement begins scary, with lurching notes for cello that suggest an encroaching fog and wind. The tones are dark and sinister, but then the music shifts as if sunlight has broken through, rising and becoming brighter as the other instruments join in. The harmonies are complex, majestic like natural forces in tension — it sounds oceanic, volcanic, but then becomes sweeter and romantic, as if it can't make up its mind what it is. Po imagined things coming to life in the morning, all god's creatures, not just great and small but chipper, dour, gentle, nasty: hippos, wolves, birds, insects, he could hear them all. These are the sounds of a rude awakening. The music isn't exactly discordant but it does get unsettling at times, especially with the rumbling drums and tympani. It's like Copland constipated, the Appalachian Spring depressed and twisted up in a fat Germanic pretzel (but then he thought this must be the Sibelius that Chelsea had mentioned — do the Finnish eat pretzels?). No one can be comfortable listening to this for more than a few seconds at a time, he thought. Chelsea wasn't the biggest fan of this bloated, uneasy music, but she thought the opening and ending of the first movement were beautiful, as well as the wonderful oboe part.

The second movement has prancing strings that give way to threatening suspense music. One might picture a pillow being pushed down into someone's face. Otherwise it's hard to visualize what the hell is going on. The third movement begins like slow moving smoke coming through the space under a door. Threat and repose alternate, hints of evil, an overall feel of methodical searching, sleepiness. There are no triumphs. It oozes. Eight minutes or so in to the movement a sustained rise begins, strength builds, the tension mounts, then there is an interlude, a sagging, followed by more uplifting, like wind in a sail. Po imagined a Viking homecoming, but then couldn't remember if Finns were Vikings (Sibelius *was* a Finn, right?); if not, then a homecoming back from the steppes or fjords or polar Las Vegas, whatever best applies. Something cold and gray yet hopeful. Then it is like sleep again with a restored sense of impending danger.

The fourth movement begins with livelier violin action, and Po enjoyed watching Chelsea do her thing here. If the first three movements were more Wagnerian, this recalled Prokoviev's Peter and the Wolf, that Russian playful quality, with standout lines for the oboe and . . . is that a glockenspiel? The bow movements for the violinists were motions like shaving or carving a steak, Po thought (he was also not yet a vegetarian). Anyway, he was more of a classic rock guy anyway and Sibelius or Dvořák or whoever this was didn't have much mercy on his listeners in this piece, as there is hardly a memorable melody anywhere. It's more like a Finnish skyscape, with thunder and rain overhead, slightly clear on the horizon, visible sun far-off on the hill, and overcast the other direction.

"Okay people," said the conductor, clapping his hands, "We're getting there! The first movement is still very sloppy, but I think you're all improving. Especially my darling oboist! Remember, it's not the notes on the page, it's the passion, it's what can't be written! We're all out of time today but there will be more Finnish fun with Sibelius next time. See you Friday! In the meantime, practice your parts!"

The musicians gathered up their sheet music, some chatted; Chelsea, who was seated in the second row in the large half-circle around the conductor, said goodbye to her fellow violinists and headed for Po, giving him a quick smile and wave with her bow before packing her violin in its case. She walked up the aisle toward him self-consciously. He tried not to stare but couldn't help himself, and couldn't help but record this moment in his memory for all time, the sight of her approaching him, the look on her face, the way she tousled her hair, her gait.

Jean Sibelius (1865-1957) is by far the world's most famous and accomplished native of Finland; the closest contender would, of course, be Huckleberry Finn, a far less

112

skilled musician and composer. Sibelius' lifetime spanned Wagner, Mahler, Stravinsky, and Prokoviev, and his music reflects these German and Russian influences plus a distinctive Nordic element all its own, as is true of the country of Finland itself.

"Hi Po, how are you? What did you think?"

"Impressive. That's a small army up there."

"Yes, next we're either going to try Beethoven's 1st symphony or invade Iwo Jima."

"Watch out, the whole troupe could get sent to Baghdad."

"Some days I'd rather be in Baghdad. You were lucky — you missed one of the rehearsals where we spend five or ten minutes on each measure, dissecting each harmony, discussing each note. It can get grueling and the conductor doesn't always handle his frustration so well."

"Plus you're almost right in his face."

"I wish I could sit in the back with the percussion and have a better view of the action, instead of staring at the conductor's nose hair."

"It reminded me of a machine, or a giant beehive. You wail on that thing . . . quite the demon with the bow, that's what it's called, right?"

"Thank you." She blushed, quietly thrilled by the

compliment. "It's not my favorite piece of music. Sibelius has had better moments. This one is so slow . . . like a water buffalo in a coma slow . . . but there are beautiful parts. I'm not sure if a normal audience will appreciate it. I'm not sure I do."

"Ah, I thought it might be the Sibelius. It changes so much."

"Right. Nothing lasts for long. This symphony is an odd choice. I like it but . . ."

"But?"

"I don't know, I feel like . . . like it has nothing to do with my life. These are emotions and images I can't relate to. And it kind of makes my stomach hurt."

"Aww, like those antacid commercials. Britney Spears does that to me."

"Hee-hee."

"What did you mean by images?"

"You know, the story and feel the composer wants to communicate."

"I'm not sure Sibelius even knew what he was feeling. Maybe that music is a lonely game of hide and seek."

"That makes more sense than you think!" Chelsea laughed, semi-nervously, and sat down in the seat directly in front of Po, sitting on her knees in the seat and holding the seat-back with both hands, almost like it was a shield but more like a child ducking over the wall of a play-fort.

"I'm secretly a music critic at night."

"When you're not at the law office?"

"After that. I only sleep on weekends."

"No extra job on the weekends?"

"No, that is my weekend job. I am a professional sleeper and dream tester."

"Aha, a dream tester! Test any good ones lately?" This was first-class flirty banter.

"There's this new one that involves falling."

"Ha. Shocking."

"And another one that involves flying."

"Cool."

"And another with both falling and flying."

"But which one comes first? So, tell me this, do you like your name?" Chelsea asked.

"Do you?"

"Yes, very much."

"Yeah, it's all right. I never liked it much when I was growing up, but at some point, I kind of liked having a, um, distinct name."

"You said it's Russian."

"Right, my grandparents came over just after World War II. My parents are still very Russian culturally. It's a strong thing back East. I guess I should be glad they didn't call me Stenka."

"That's a name?"

"Sure. Could you imagine the taunts? Hey, stinky, stenchy . . . "

"Stinkpants, stinkbreath, Comrade Stank."

"Good one. The other possibility was Ilya."

"Lil' Illin' Ilya, I can hear it now. So you weren't teased, Porfiry?"

"No, not much. 'Po' is strong, kind of cool, and poverty is a virtue, right?"

"It is?"

"Yeah, didn't you get the memo from Jesus?"

"Maybe—did it say something like 'you may have already won one hundred thousand dollars from publisher's clearing house,' with all these magazine stickers and a picture of God wearing glasses on the front?"

"That's it!" They chuckled together.

"I hate stickers," Po said.

"You do!" Chelsea lit up even more. "I can't stand them! Stickers everywhere."

"Ugh."

"Double ugh." She could very easily love a man who hated stickers, and apparently already did. "Did you know the orchestra is going to St. Petersburg?"

"You mean Russia and not Florida?"

"That's right."

"Cool. Cold. Say, what do you call it when violinists pluck the strings with their fingers?"

"Is that a joke? You mean opposed to their feet? Am I supposed to guess the punch line?"

"No, I'm serious. I like it."

"Oh, that's called *Pizzicato*."

"Pizzicato, all right." Po liked learning things and smiled with contentment.

"So, Po, you had more questions to ask me about Mrs. Andrews?"

"Who? Oh, that. No, not really. In the law game we call that 'false pretense.'"

"Ha. So what is your sordid plan?"

"I don't know, coffee? Tea? Ice cream?"

"Ooh, I like that last one."

"A woman after my own heart. Let's get out of here."

"Great." Chelsea stood up to leave, looking around for her things.

"Do you have everything?"

"I think so." As she grabbed her hippie-looking purse, the telltale Ziploc bag of crushed peanuts fell out, in one of those frozen instances we all know. Po and Chelsea both stared at the bag and then each other, then Chelsea scrambled to scoop the bag into her purse. "Uh, that's not what you think."

"Not heroin?"

"Ha, no."

"Hash?"

"No."

"Damn, 'cause I'm all out." This relieved a nervous tension. Another nice play by Po. Don't we all have skeletons or mysterious Ziploc bags in the closet?

"Would you believe me if I said it was a bag of crushed peanuts?"

"Can I see?"

"Sure." She reached into her purse and handed him the bag.

"Yeah, those are crushed nuts all right. Now is that a proper snack, Miss Walker? Or did you have an incident with an elephant?"

"Ha. I hate the shells and skins and I have sensitive teeth, you know."

"Sure. Fillings?"

"You know it. Ouch." She made a cute little grimace and then smiled and hoped he wasn't good at spotting lies. Damn, she didn't want to start out dishonestly with him. He sensed something was up, but what else could she possibly have crushed peanuts for, unless this was some new drug fad he was unaware of. Snorting almonds. These kids today, though, who knows . . .

"Isn't there a type of nut called a Filbert?" he asked as they were walking up towards the exits.

"I think so."

"Ever see one?"

"I'm not sure. You?"

"Maybe, I don't know. If so, it didn't leave much of an impression."

"Poor Filbert."

chapter eighteen

frodo, fonzie, j. edgar

They walked over to the ice cream parlor on campus, Frodo's, which was designed and decorated not to evoke Middle Earth, as the name suggests, but rather 1950s America, with chrome-sided Formica and red plastic booths. In the corner was a very large jukebox stuffed with hoary ditties from Red Scare days gone by, on real vinyl records. The time-warp was thrown by coeds glazed-eyed in front of their laptops, others gabbing on call-phones or texting.

As they walked in, Po remarked, "Whoah. They should call this Fonzie's instead of Frodo's."

"Who?" Chelsea asked.

"Fonzie—you know, from *Happy Days*, that sit-com." Po really hadn't felt old up until this point, and he remembered that he was with a 19 year-old girl.

"Oh, yeah, I've seen that. A really, really bad show. From the '70s, right, but set in the '50s? Fonzie is that cool guy with the jacket and the thumbs." She did the double ayyyyy, which, needless to say, was adorable.

"That's the one, and that was very cute. Why do they call this Frodo's if it's all '50s memorabilia?"

"Beats me. I never really thought about it. Maybe the name came first. Let me ask." By this time one of the college-age workers in white apron and goofy hat—"Steve," according to his nametag—was standing at the counter ready to take their order.

"Hi, what can I get you?'

"Why is this place called Frodo's?" Chelsea inquired.

He blankly stared off to the side and repeated a familiar refrain, in a listless monotone: "Frodo's was originally called Frodo's Frozen Delights. The original owner's name was Frederick Douglas, and his wife used to call him Frodo. They first met in 1957 in a malt shop that looked like this one." *Drone* is both a noun and a verb.

"You mean Frederick Douglass, like the abolitionist Frederick Douglass?" Po half-joked.

"Huh?" Steve the soda jerk had not a clue. Po didn't know that much more about Frederick Douglass either, so he left it at that.

"Forget it. So, what would you like, Chelsea?"

"Hmm, ahh, how about a hot fudge sundae?"

"Should we split one?"

"Ooh, yay!" So romantic! She wondered if this was heaven. Maybe she had smothered herself accidentally.

"How big?"

"Extra *extra*."

Counter boy Steve chimed in here: "Three scoops in the big cup? What flavors?"

Chelsea and Po decided on mocha, coconut, and cookie dough, an excellent trio, definitely with the whipped cream.

"I guess we don't need nuts, since you brought your own," Po said.

Chelsea laughed a bit uneasily at this. "Ha, right, no nuts."

They plopped themselves down at a booth. Po looked around and studied the wall decorations: posters for old 1950s products, magazine photos of 1950s Hollywood stars and sports figures, the obligatory Marilyn Monroe shrine, and so on. There was one of Marilyn with Arthur Miller — such a strange pairing, Po thought, as if Paris Hilton and Stephen Hawking hooked up. What did they ever talk about? Did they ever talk? Was he perchance the love of her life? Did she think about Arthur Miller or Joe DiMaggio when she was banging the Kennedy brothers?

He decided it was best not to be thinking so much about sex on a first date.

"Ah, the golden age of hula hoops and white cotton t-shirts. I guess we're spoiling dinner. What would your Mom say?"

"I don't know where you come from, but where I come from there have always been special rules for ice cream," Chelsea replied warmly.

"Ha, me too. Ice cream is one of the few truly good things in this world. I've always said, when babies are born and are crying, the doctors should, um, whisper in their ears 'It's all right, there's ice cream.'" He whispered the last part for effect.

"Awww," Chelsea thought this was irresistible, that it should be part of wedding vows also, but thought it better to keep that thought to herself. "Right, I wouldn't say to them, 'It's all right there's George W. Bush looking out for you,' or 'It's ok, there's botox.'"

"Or get ready, there's cigarettes and high fructose corn syrup and flesh-eating bacteria."

"They could say to the babies, 'It's Miller Time!'"

"Ha!"

"So you don't smoke?"

"No."

"Good. My friend Carrie does. I really hate it."

"My mother smoked . . . still does, I guess . . . and she had a heat attack when she was 45."

"Wow, so young."

"Yeah. Just a weakness of the will, I suppose."

"And culture. In the 1950s, everyone smoked, right?"

"And wore suits and hats, all the time."

"And the women wore dresses.'

"So did J. Edgar Hoover."

"Huh? Wasn't he President during the depression."

Po again felt a bit old, or at least over-educated. "No, that's Herbert Hoover, as in sherbet. J. Edgar Hoover was the cross-dressing director of the FBI."

"Oh right, that sounds familiar. Zombie Commies and all that."

"Uh, right. Look at the women on the walls. They had such a different shape back then. I wonder why."

Chelsea felt self-conscious about her appearance, as she herself was a tad full-figured, let's say, not a bad body by any means, but certainly not a gaunt, leggy, big-breasted supermodel. "Different brassiers and girdles, I suppose. And people exercise more now."

"Look how their hips are so round and jut out, and the, um, breasts so pointy." Po could see the attraction for sweaters, long skirts, and ponytails, though. He imagined Chelsea dressed in such an outfit, then undressed, and again told himself to stop thinking about sex.

"Those were the days," Chelsea remarked, interrupting his fantasy.

"Oh, I'm sorry, I guess this isn't the best conversation topic."

"I don't mind."

Just then the soda jerk arrived with the sundae, an elaborate mound with a decadent amount of fudge, a cloudbank of whipped cream, plus cherry on top, all in a stainless steel boat, accompanied by two spoons.

"Whoah," Po said as the sundae slid near him. "Where have you been all my life?"

Chelsea grabbed a spoon and leaned forward. "Do you mean the sundae or me?"

He smiled. "Both." Their eyes met, metaphysically and every other way. "All right, let's do it."

Anyone eavesdropping on the session that followed (such as the poor freckle-faced kid in the striped shirt seated in the next booth), would have then heard certain very male and female sounds: deep moans of delight, passionate oohs and ahs, lip-smacking, and the unmistakable sounds of quasi-sexual ecstasy as induced by this full-bodied ice cream and luscious melted fudge. Needless to say, their taste buds were completely

125

aroused. Po wondered if the '50s jukebox had Ravel's *Boléro*, and if he might take Chelsea right there on the Formica table-top. Could he last the fifteen minutes of the *Boléro* — that is, until the unabashedly orgasmic, elephantine ending of the composition? Or would it be more like the approximately two minutes of "Rock Around the Clock" — or perhaps more appropriately, "Great Balls of Fire"? So far his attempt to not think about sex wasn't exactly a resounding success.

"So, tell me," Chelsea began to say, as Po reached over and wiped off stray fudge from her lower lip with his finger, while she closed her eyes and basked in the feeling, "why do you want to be a lawyer? Do you love the law?"

"No, I wouldn't say that. Maybe I'll love it more after I pass the bar. I guess I'd say, um, that I believe in it, though. I know too much about it to love it. Do you? Do musicians even have to worry about it, aside from the occasional drug or peanut bust?"

"Ha. Well, sometimes, I don't know. I wouldn't call myself an anarchist, but I think justice and fairness are more than just law. It's different. Law isn't good by definition. There are good laws and some that are just there, maybe just meant to be annoying. Like the government is flexing its muscle, and that's how it does that. I mean, I'd have to think about each law. And then there's mercy, which I'd say is higher than justice, because it has forgiveness and love."

"Right, but our system sort of has mercy built into it. Law gives it structure."

Hmm, Chelsea thought vaguely, *I think the law just makes it impersonal and kills it,* but she wasn't confident enough in this idea to express it.

Counter boy/soda jerk/waiter Steve came back with two enormous glasses of water and set them down in front of Chelsea and Po. "Do you two like jokes?"

"No, we hate jokes," Chelsea answered.

"You're kidding, right?" Steve was evidently a bit slow.

"Right."

"Okay, an iguana walks into a bar and says, 'I'd like a beer.' The bartender says, 'We don't serve iguanas.' So the iguana says, 'Well, your Mom did.'"

There was an uneasy silence. Chelsea and Po looked at each other, waiting for each other to laugh, to see who would crack first, then seemed to mutually understand that this was a fine time to tease the joke-teller.

"I don't get it," Po said.

"No? Really?" Steve sincerely believed that an explanation might help. "You see, it's a talking animal joke, but it becomes a 'your mom' joke."

"Oh, so it's funny because animals can't talk. Do

127

iguanas drink beer?" Chelsea asked, with feigned befuddlement.

"Uh, I don't know. It doesn't matter. He could have ordered a seltzer."

"So," Po interjected, "is the implication that the bartender's mother had intercourse with an iguana? How is that even possible?"

"Ah, you two are just playing with me." Then Chelsea and Po couldn't help but burst at the seams, laughing boisterously — partially at the joke, partially at how poorly it was told, most of all at how poorly it was explained. Steve was slightly offended but couldn't help but to enjoy the response, the joy of it.

After savoring every last spoonful of ice cream and every drop of chocolate, Po and Chelsea went for a walk around campus. After a few strides he reached down to hold her hand, and she gladly took it, without looking at him, as if they had been holding hands all their lives and it was the most natural of things; both felt a jolt of electricity that felt amazingly unique and yet so familiar at the same time. They sat down next to the campus fountain, and at 7:27 pm PDT, the sky a lavender dusk, they shared their first kiss, which was tender, long, very loving, and was instantly followed by another that was even better.

Human beings in the initial stages of mating send various cues signaling interest and receptivity, often preceded by the over-consumption of alcohol. The potential partners will place their heads at a directional angle, slightly bowed toward each other; the pupils dilate and breath quickens, while the dorsal fin increases in temperature and the gullet tightens; this is followed by lip lubrication and then the "kissy face," kind of a googly stare accompanied by a heavy, anticipatory silence that says to the other, "kiss me, you fool." Lips touch, tongues search for each other, hands start finding their way to pet and caress certain places, and the journey of mutual discovery begins. This then leads to a second, more overt set of signals: for instance, Chelsea felt her female parts flutter and Po had a rocket in his pocket, or in that general vicinity.

chapter nineteen

girls

Back at home that night, as Chelsea was brushing her teeth and getting ready for bed, Darlene appeared, jealous and a bit miffed. "I could meet someone, too, you know."

"Hm?"

"I could meet someone. I could."

Chelsea was feeling good and was in no mood for Darlene's antics. "Really? How does that work? Where would you go? A Club Med vacation to someone else's shoulder? Maybe to the kneecap? Fabulous getaway to the patella!"

Darlene folded her arms in real irritation. "Don't you think he's kind of . . . *old* . . . for you?"

"No, I don't think so. I'd say he's probably 27 or 28, right? And his name is Po, you could call him by his name."

"Right, Russian mafia, I forgot. When he graduated

high school, you were 10 years old. What was the name of your favorite dolly? Remember how big the big kids looked back then? How many women—*women*, not girls—do you think he's been with?"

"Doesn't love transcend time?"

"Ha, yeah, right. Woody and Soon Yi forever."

"Why not?"

"You handled the peanut thing well."

"I am picking up on your sarcasm, Darlene."

"Good. I wonder if he is out trawling the middle schools right now looking for another date. 'Hey little girls, want to see a grown man's whiskers? I have candy. And roofies.' You should ask him how old his previous girlfriend was, if she wore braces and a training bra."

"Please shut up."

"And how come he's never been married? I bet he has herpes. Isn't it interesting, also, that the only reason you met him was because you were hanging around the old folks' home, looking for another elderly crusty betty to smother? How romantic."

"Darlene!"

"I just think it's funny. Are you going to tell him about your little, *ahem,* shipping spree?"

"I'm not talking to you anymore."

"He might be a bit surprised to hear about your *experience,* eh? So much for the innocent virgin non-homicidal dream."

With that remark Chelsea reached over and angrily flicked Darlene with her finger off into the corner of the room. "Leave me alone. I'm going to bed."

"C'mon, why did you do that? Ow, goddamnit. Hey, don't forget tomorrow's Saturday and we're taking care of the geek!" Darlene brushed herself off, sat by the wall, and steamed and sulked while Chelsea slept. "Love is shit," the shoulder devil muttered under her breath.

♪ ♪ ♪

In the morning Chelsea had breakfast with her mother — croissants and fresh fruit — and told her about her magical first date with Po. Chelsea was glowing. It is interesting how *liberating* becoming involved with someone can feel. If nothing else, this man had freed from her any kind of emotional dependence on college boys, few of whom were worthy of any kind of love at all and certainly not hers.

"Did he kiss you?"

"Mom!"

"Well?" she asked again, slyly, giggling.

"Yes! For a long time. It was wonderful. By the fountain on campus, after we shared an ice cream sundae together. The sky was beautiful. He has such loving eyes, such an amazing touch."

"Ooh! I bet he is a good kisser." Chelsea smiled at her mother's comment, proud of this triumph. Her mother, meanwhile, dreamily imagined herself kissing Po, but she pushed that out of her mind quickly, then wondered exactly how far her daughter would go on the first date with an older man, with all the expectations that there might be. Thinking is a whole mess of trouble, she thought.

"What time did you get in last night? I must have already been asleep. I didn't hear a thing."

"Oh, midnight, or 1, something like that. Not too late. He has to work this morning."

"On a Saturday? He's such a busy man, it seems. When do you think you are going to see him again?"

"Maybe tonight. I need to rehearse for the funeral tomorrow, though, and I have a paper to write for English class for Monday."

"We should invite him over to dinner next week. Wouldn't that be nice? After you two have had more time alone. We could cook something together."

"I think he'd like that. I told him you have a crush on

him."

"Oh, please. But you could ask him if he knows any single men in their late 40s! Or younger, I don't mind. Maybe a lawyer. We could double date."

"Oh my god, Mom."

"What? It's just a thought. I'm still alive!"

Meanwhile, Po was sending Chelsea an e-mail:

Dear Chelsea

I had a great time last night (an understatement) and would like to see you again. Just say when. I have to say that I've never felt kisses like that before: they were exactly how I always imagined kisses should be. You take my breath away. You should give lessons, or train yourself in CPR just in case my heart explodes next time.

You even make the 1950s special.

— Po

p.s. Oh, I thought of a joke, almost as good as Steve's. A duck walks into the bar. Before he can speak, the bartender says, "Hey, let me guess, you want a beer and I should put it on your bill." The duck responds, "Hey, eat shit, asshole." So should I give up the law and become a comedy writer?

*p.p.s.   And that's the duck's dirty language, not
mine. I would wash his mouth out with duck soap.*

Reading over this note, and recognizing how much he had
already fallen for this 19 year-old, he said out loud to himself
with a self-satisfied tone, "Well, Po, old boy, if love doesn't drive
you completely insane, what good is it?"

♪ ♪ ♪

There was still the issue of exactly how to dispatch
Gerald—a foolproof way to rid herself of the fool, as it were—
and Chelsea was still tinkering with the plan. She found it hard
to concentrate, as she kept thinking of Po, trying hard not to
become mired in the doubts that Darlene raised. She sent him a
quick e-mail, *2night maybe? I'll call after rehearsal. I am certified in
First Aid. Have fun (and mischief) at work. Miss you. P.S. foul-
mouthed duck jokes=humor.* Okay, focus, she said, and she sat in
her "thinking chair," a gloriously ratty goodwill special, a
recliner that no longer reclined but still felt like sitting in the
Buddha's lap—that is, not the Buddha, but Guanyin, the obese
Chinese bodhisattva and god of wealth that many people
confuse for the historical Buddha. Siddhartha Gautama is the

thin, contemplative, obviously enlightened Buddha, not some fat money-grubbing shit. I can picture Guanyin holding a bag of pork rinds and 40-ouncer, with cookie crumbs in his navel, but not Siddhartha.

Okay, think, think, think: Chelsea tried to conceive of a way to not actually be there with Gerald when the deed was happening and the nuts taking effect, but it seemed impossible to avoid. They were set to meet late afternoon to practice a few songs. Chelsea's goal was to get rid of him today before tomorrow's funeral and keep all that filthy lucre for herself. Here was the plan—at practice, she would slip him one of her mom's diuretic tablets in his water bottle, during one of the many instances when he closes his eyes in rapture while playing the accordion. After an hour or so, she would invite him out to a late lunch or early dinner, her treat. Gerald would jump at the chance to spend quality time with her, as he was a teenage boy and generally lonely, and she was collegiate cool—he wouldn't be doing anything on a Saturday night except watching *Doctor Who* and possibly pulling the pork. (or even more likely, pulling the latter while watching the former). She would take him to a place downtown known for its chili and soup. The diuretic would ensure at least one trip to the bathroom, if not several. When Gerald was away from the table relieving his watery bladder, Chelsea would then empty the crushed peanuts into his chili or soup. Chelsea also considered sneaking him a beer at rehearsal, but she couldn't be sure that he would drink it. Gerald didn't strike her as a fella who appreciated Miller Time: he would probably go into an Irish pub and order a mojito or mai tai. Anyway, alcohol in his system would be very suspicious, so she would stick with the diuretic pill. She doubted that the diuretic would be traceable, as it would likely just get pissed out, but it was over-the-counter anyway, a normal dietary supplement for those wanting to shed a few pounds, and wouldn't necessarily need to be explained. Teens will be teens. Besides, any coroner worth his salt would quickly see all the indications of peanut poisoning and leave it at that. Chelsea imagined the restaurant owner, Claude Boles (also the director of the community theater) being interviewed on television afterwards: "Well, there were no nuts in that particular recipe, but in a kitchen, alas, things happen. Our deepest condolences go out to the young man's family in the face of this terrible tragedy. It was a very unfortunate accident that demonstrates the fleeting quality of life . . . and we pray to the good Lord in heaven above that we don't get sued just because of a few stinkin' filberts." Chelsea laughed, remembering Po's filbert reference.

The memorial service the next day was for a Mrs. Gladys McDaniel Rosenbaum, one of the nursing home residents that

Chelsea had snuffed out recently. Chelsea thought she might be the one with the moustache and Parkinson's, and she was half-right. Her husband was Ira Rosenbaum, the town podiatrist, still practicing at the spry old age of 68, the son of a Holocaust survivor. Rumors were that Dr. Rosenbaum had a foot fetish that wouldn't quit. He was known for his very attentive treatment of bunions and fallen arches. Mrs. Rosenbaum was originally an Irish Catholic who had converted when she and Ira married. She surprised everyone by specifying in her will that she wanted to be buried with full Catholic rites. "I'm sick of this Jewish nonsense," she wrote, apparently not realizing that Christianity began as a Jewish sect, that the very idea of Jesus was a Jewish one, and thus the core nonsense was all Jewish. It turns out that most religious conversions are due to marriage, as statistics overwhelmingly confirm, presumably motivated by other factors besides the Holy Spirit or the logical persuasiveness of the various creeds. When the couple had met, many moons ago, Ira was an up and coming professional, a good doctor with a large, disease-free penis, while most of the men Gladys knew in her church were drunken Irish manual laborers, the occasional mick police officer or barkeep, and second generation Mexican immigrants whose families had saved enough money to move into town from the farm camps. Anyway, to accommodate both sides of the family, an interesting set was planned for the service:

Ave Maria; When Irish Eyes are Smiling, and Chelsea actually regretted that she wouldn't have the accordion accompaniment for this one, as it would sound much better with it; and then, by special request, a mournful version of *Hava Nagila,* that would then build up and be more suited to an Irish wake-type of atmosphere. Chelsea wasn't sure how it would go, but she was fairly certain there'd be potato pancakes.

♪ ♪ ♪

Gerald and Chelsea met to rehearse at one of the practice rooms in the music building. Like any high schooler, Gerald was excited to be on campus and tried to act cooler than usual so not to be spotted as an obvious interloper. He said things like "Yeah, whatever, man," not part of his usual patois. Chelsea was in the lobby when he arrived, her violin in its case, nuts in her shoulder bag.

"Well, hello, Chelsea. We meet again. I see you couldn't live without me."

"Indeed. Are you ready to rock?"

Gerald, who was wearing polar-gray lenses still dark from the sun and a hooded sweatshirt (or "hoodie"), obligatory college camouflage in the Northwest, patted his accordion case. "Always," he replied. Somewhere angels groaned.

"I brought the sheet music for you for *Hava Nagila* and *Irish Eyes*, if you need it."

"Yeah, whatever, man. Let's jam."

Chelsea couldn't help herself and said, "Right on," but *Rest in Peace Geek* was what she thought. Right dead.

Everything went according to plan, with nary a hitch. The windowless practice room was rather stuffy, as they tend to be, and accordion playing is rather physical, so Gerald was glad that Chelsea had brought an extra bottle of water for him. He drank from it often, almost every pause as they worked on the songs. He made no comment about the taste, so the diuretic mickey seemingly had dissolved well. After the third run through of Hava Nagila, Gerald happily accepted the lunch invitation and the prospect of walking downtown with an attractive coed. He insisted on ordering the "Five Alarm Habanero Death Chili," which Chelsea immediately realized was the best possible choice—the initial reaction would be that the spicy food did him and his own recklessness in and not any concealed nuts. Perhaps this was the best of all possible worlds.

It was quite a commotion at the restaurant after everything went down; there weren't that many people there to start, but once the sirens started getting closer and the police and ambulance arrived, a curious crowd rapidly materialized at the epicenter. CPR failed to revive the victim. Chelsea had to give her phone number to the police just in case they had any questions, although the detective at the scene, Lieutenant Jones, said that it seemed to him like an "open and shut" case of either a hot pepper-induced coronary or possibly food allergies, given the swelling, rash, apparent asphyxiation, the chili stains on his shirt, and all the signs of anaphylactic shock. "I guess that boy just couldn't handle the heat," he concluded. "Five alarm chili was one or two alarms too many for the little guy." Chelsea wasn't sure what the anaphylactic shock meant and neither was the detective, but that's what the EMTs had told him. It's like Gerald's own body strangled him, he explained to Chelsea. "I'm surprised it waited this long," an exuberant Darlene quipped; thankfully Chelsea managed to keep a straight face.

"Was he your boyfriend?" Jones asked.

"No, no, just a friend. An acquaintance, really. We play, uh, concerts together sometimes. I play violin. He's an accordionist," Chelsea responded.

"Ah." It was as if that explained everything.

"We were practicing today then took a break to get a bite to eat."

I guess the food bit him, Jones thought. Over the years he had learned to keep things like this to himself. "An awful thing," he said.

The detective then called Gerald's mother. Chelsea

could hear wailing on the phone from several feet away. Oh well.

The restaurant owner, Mr. Boles, arrived to do damage control, from God knows where. He was wearing a bright green tank top and blue bicycle shorts, which accentuated the flabbiness and flatness of his ass, an odd outfit considering how unseasonably cold it was. It occurred to Chelsea that there should be age limits or age specifications for bicycle shorts, like the ones they have for children's toys: "not suitable for children under four," etc., except it should be "bicycle shorts inappropriate attire for adults over the age of 50." And there should be some related restriction against his very thick salt and pepper shoulder hair. Of the mentality that no publicity is bad publicity, Boles was already mulling over a "Death Chili Challenge" contest or something like that when the time was right, once the community had gotten over its initial shock and had time to grieve; it could be a big to-do with doctors on the scene and waiters dressed like ghosts or skeletons. He saw this attracting not only chili and hot pepper aficionados, of course, but also macho men and thrill seekers as a food equivalent of extreme sports, plus all the frat dudes in town. For the time being, however, it would have to be taken off the menu while the police and health inspectors confirmed it wasn't poisoned or anything. Yellow "police line—do not cross" tape was put around the soup and chili tureens. "I run a tight ship," Mr. Boles kept telling anyone that would listen. "Don't worry about anything. The food is safe. Our chili will rise again."

Chelsea was kind of disappointed that Gerald was wheeled off on a stretcher with a sheet over his face and hoodie instead of being zipped up into a body bag. Chelsea had imagined the sound of it beforehand and felt, in a word, *cheated* of the proper experience—not that she was delighting in this, not at all. But she did have certain auditory expectations as a musician and now things seemed a bit off. Walking back to campus to fetch her violin (and Gerald's accordion, she hadn't accounted for that previously), she sent a text message to Po saying that there was a medial emergency, a friend of hers had an accident and that she couldn't hang out tonight, but Monday she would have time after her classes. Po wondered if she might have another date or something but then decided to take her at her word. "Mistrust is no way to start a relationship," he advised himself. *And what kind of person would lie about a medical emergency?* Another Saturday night's hope dashed, the void to be filled yet again with something or other. He had even washed his sheets and made his bed and checked the expiration date on the condoms tucked away in his nightstand, hoping for a young visitor, just in case, because things happen and a guy needs to be ready. His fallback was to go play poker with some

143

of his colleagues from work—they had a weekly low stakes Texas Hold 'Em game on Saturday nights, but he was already very tired of the whole thing and felt much closer to Chelsea after two days than any of them after two years. Poker meant four or five hours of sitting, drinking, smoking, snacking, and listening to all their bullshit yet again (as if during the week wasn't enough), assuming he didn't go bust early, which was almost a blessing.

Chelsea went home, told her mother the news, and then decided it would be best if she acted sullen and stunned. Several hours later Gerald's mother called the house to commiserate. She and Chelsea's mother spoke for a long time, and then she asked to speak to Chelsea.

"Hi Chelsea."

"Hi Mrs. Edwards. I'm so sorry for your loss. I wish I could have done something. I can't believe he's gone."

"Thank you, sweetheart," she said, choking back sobs. "I always told Gerald to make sure there were no nuts whenever he went out to eat. I'm surprised he didn't."

Chelsea said nothing.

"But I guess it is all the same now. . . . Chelsea, Gerald's father and I need to start making arrangements for the . . . and we both know how fond Gerald was of you. I'm sure he would want you to play at the memorial service. He loved music so much and I know how much he enjoyed the times he performed with you."

Darlene could barely contain herself. Chelsea answered, "I would be honored, Mrs. Edwards."

"It will be late next week, I think, I'd say Friday. I need to call the school, tell his teachers. My God, this is awful."

"Yes, it is."

"My little baby is gone."

Cheslea wasn't sure what to say, so she made something up. "I'm sure he is in heaven now, Mrs. Edwards. He's in a better place."

Gerald's mother was close to completely breaking down. Her husband, Mitch, standing there beside her, put his arm around her and said, "There, there." She could barely hold up the phone any longer and struggled to get out the words, "Thank you so much, Chelsea." Click.

chapter twenty

flirp and blerf, robert frost and merv

The Rosenbaum service was an early afternoon affair. Both the Micks and the Heebs were on good behavior, and the children present, being children, all seemed to get along. Perhaps none had yet been conditioned to be alcoholic racists or to think they were the chosen people. Chelsea sensed there could be more love matches from among this mix. Inspired by the warm, hopeful gathering, she played violin beautifully and received many compliments. Dr. Rosenbaum said she had nice feet.

The essay Chelsea had to write for her English class that weekend was on the question of whether the unexamined life is worth living. Socrates supposedly said no. Socrates himself never sat down to write an essay, so we can only guess as to what he thought, based on the second-hand accounts of two of his students, Plato and Xenophon, and the comic playwright

Aristophanes, a contemporary and fellow Athenian who felt Socrates was a charlatan/mountebank/scoundrel who had his head in the clouds and talked out of his ass (thus the title of Aristophanes' play, *The Clouds*, and the unpublished sequel, *Asstalker*). Chelsea reflected on this view of the unexamined life — examined it, as it were — and decided that it was exactly the kind of thing a philosopher might say. Moreover, it seemed to justify disregarding the lives of other creatures and non-philosophically inclined humans, which had disturbing implications. If those lives aren't worth living, does it follow that those beings are worth killing, that their lives can be or should be sacrificed for the sake of those that are more intellectually or perhaps spiritually valuable? Chelsea wasn't opposed to killing *per se*, obviously, but her selection for victims had nothing to do with the capacity for self-examination. There was nothing intellectual about any of it. More importantly, what did philosophy have to do with love? Music? Dancing? The main thrust of her thesis became the notion that the unloved life was not worth living, that examination only has value if it leads to loving actions. She decided to title her essay "Publish or Perish? Defending the Unexamined Life" which she thought her instructor might like.

Carrie, meanwhile, in her paper was arguing that *no* life was worth living. Existence was purely accidental and questions of value were meaningless and absurd. We could never have the perspective of eternity to determine such things, so such speculations were pointless, since one could always argue the opposite of whatever was posed. It was completely arbitrary to separate the goats from the sheep or at least it wasn't some metaphysical mandate. In certain contexts dying could have much more value than living. While to certain perspectives suicide is a cardinal sin, to others it is an act of heroism or exalted martyrdom. Something like that. Jesus basically committed suicide instead of using his cosmic superpowers to resist the Romans. He could have turned their blood to water, killing them instantly, and then to wine, and so forth.

Chelsea was about halfway done her paper on Sunday night when Po called, their first official phone conversation. She was excited and nervous to see his name in the caller ID screen of her cell phone.

"Hello?"

"Hi, it's Po."

"Hi!"

"How is everything?"

"Fine, I played a funeral today, been working on my essay that's due tomorrow."

"A nice time, the funeral I mean? Well, the essay, too, I guess." Po was well aware of how stupid this was already sounding. He didn't think much of his phone skills to begin with — although certain ex-girlfriends would talk his ear off on the telephone, this was more about their needs (and his patience) than his charm.

"It was a good service — Irish/Jewish."

"That's interesting." His mind ran through possible jokes here but decided they were too risky: *What did you play? Hava O'Nagila? Something from Fiddler on the Dole? Or Fiddler on the Sauce? Potato on the Roof?* Nah.

"That's exactly right. Interesting." She chuckled even though nothing humorous had been said. And that seemed funny to her.

"And writing a paper, eh?"

"Yes, about whether the unexamined life is worth living."

"Ah. What's the answer?"

"So far I have written, 'Woof woof woof.'"

"Ha. Well, keep at it. Don't forget *whinny whinny*."

"Right."

"And oink oink moo moo snurt."

"Hee-hee. What's snurt?"

"You don't know snurt?"

"Is that some barnyard animal I'm not familiar with? Old McDonald and here a snurt? Is it a zebu? I know, an ibex!"

"Once you've figured it out you will have unlocked the mystery of the unexamined life. Well, that and flirp."

"Flirp?"

"And blerf."

"Blerf I know. I wasn't born yesterday."

"You weren't?"

"No."

"Neither was I."

"No, when were you born?"

"Friday night, when we kissed."

"Aww." It was so corny that it was cute. She giggled.

"You dove right into that one!"

"I know. I was born tomorrow."

"Really?"

"Right. I'm actually late to go pick up my time machine. It's in the shop."

"That's very deep. What's wrong with it?"

"Oh, you know quantum mechanics. Probably termites."

"I have a time machine, too. But it only goes forward in one second intervals."

"Ha, the old Timex 2000. I used to have one of those."

"So how is your friend?"

"Friend?"

With this reaction of hers he wondered again if it had been a fib. "The one who had the medical emergency the other day?"

"Oh yeah. More of an acquaintance, really, but we play music together. I'm afraid he didn't make it."

"Didn't make what? Oh, you mean he died?" Po felt like a complete dolt.

"We were eating lunch and he had some sort of reaction to the spicy chili at Boles', I guess."

"Wow. That's incredible. Was he your age?"

"Younger. Just fifteen."

"Man. I saw something about that in the newspaper today, I didn't put two and two together. So you were there, you saw it?"

"I was sitting right next to him, actually. The paramedics came, police, everything."

"Intense. Scary. I'm glad you didn't eat the chili. Had you ever seen someone die before?"

She thought it wise to lie here. "Uh, no, not really. Just TV, you know."

"Me neither. Wow. I guess it wouldn't be cool for me to ask you out for tomorrow."

"No, I'd actually appreciate the distraction. I can't sit here and think about death all day. What did you have in mind?"

"What would you like to do?"

"I don't know. There's the usual dinner-movie-whatever dating thing."

"How about I think of something creative and then surprise you?"

"That sounds fun. We could so something artistic, that could be cool."

"Shh, I said a surprise. No speculatin'"

"Okay," she laughed.

"All right, I should let you get back to writing."

"Many more woofs to go before I sleep . . . "

"Good old Robert Frost—he actually was the inspiration for Scooby Doo."

"I thought that was Ezra Pound. Didn't Robert Frost play the dog on 'Frasier'?"

"Ha. Well, Godspeed, sugar."

"Sugar?" This really made her giggle.

"Right, do you like it? I thought I'd try out a term of endearment."

"Nice. Bye, Paprika."

"Paprika?"

"Right. Better than 'snookums.'"

"I like it. My mailman calls me snookums, so I guess we

should avoid any confusion. Well, I think this is where I say goodbye."

"I know it's the hardest part."

"You can call me later if you finish early."

"I will, if I can."

"Bye Chelsea."

"Bye Po."

Chelsea hung up the phone, beaming, thinking she would likely remember this conversation for the rest of her life. Po, inclined to judge and grade himself harshly, rated it a solid A-minus after a clumsy beginning. She was the star of this one, the brightest star in this dark night all around him. So much hope. And to think how cute she was being after her friend died right in front of her. This was a woman he could marry, he felt that, maybe for the first time in his life. Now he turned to the task of brainstorming, to come up with a fun, creative, and memorable date that avoided any standard boring norms and would knock this girl's socks off. Hmm . . . socks . . .

♪ ♪ ♪

The County Medical Examiner, Merv Kalinsky, was in the process of determining exactly what was in the secret recipe of Boles' "Five Alarm Habanero Death Chili" from the sample taken out of the restaurant, and comparing that with the contents of Gerald Edwards' stomach. Most he could identify under a microscope but for the spices he had to use the ol' finger and tongue method. The lab results on the whole were quite interesting:

Chili: Green peppers, jalapeño peppers, habanero peppers. Onions (white and brown). Cumin, of course. Garlic. Cilantro. Chili powder, several different kinds, including ancho. Tremendous amounts of salt. A little sugar, surprisingly. Kidney beans, garbanzo beans, red beans, lentils (red and yellow). Beef, pork, and—drum roll—small game, specifically squirrel meat. If that wasn't the secret ingredient, Kalinsky concluded, then I don't know what is.

Gerald's stomach: Oatmeal residue, presumably his breakfast from that day, plus the unmistakable radioactive glow of Lil' Sandee's brand snack cakes. And more recently, Boles' Chili, semen (Merv's own, another story for another time), and what appeared to be small undigested chunks of peanuts, which Kalinsky did not recall being in the larger chili sample. Curious. He double-checked. Hmm . . . could the squirrel also explain the nuts? Maybe. Did he care enough to check this all out? Was the kid allergic to the nuts and not the peppers? Are some people allergic to squirrel meat? Merv ate a raccoon once, but that was

154

on a dare when he was a kid.

♪ ♪ ♪

As it was approaching eleven, Chelsea was tiring and realized she may not finish her assignment, or that would be on the rough side and possibly shit, so she decided to e-mail the teacher to explain the circumstances.

> *Ms. Gardner,*
>
> *Hi, this is Chelsea from your MWF 10 am section. I'm writing my paper but I just wanted to let you know that it might be a little late and that this might not be my best work. A friend of mine died on Saturday when I was eating lunch with him at Boles' downtown. I'm dealing with it okay but it has been a little distracting . . . but I guess examining life is part of the essay, and death comes with the territory. Thank you for your time and understanding. See you in class.*

Gerald was thus raised to *friend* status in death, a place he had never officially attained in life. Perhaps someday he would become a god. Good for him. At the very least, Chelsea thought, she'd get a little extra sympathy from her anorexic feminist hard-ass teacher (who in her toughness was clearly overcompensating for being a fairly young woman and borderline imbecile, as most English grad students were at Chelsea's college) and presumably a better grade. Your life was not given in vain, Gerald. Plus she had $150 from the Rosenbaum funeral, including tips, all to herself. Maybe she'd buy Po a gift.

In a pinch, with an exam or paper deadline encroaching, many undergraduates turn to the old my grandfather or grandmother died excuse, knowing it was very unlikely that a professor would have the gall to actually try to confirm this, to request some kind of official note. It was getting to be a running joke among the students, as in "hey, Sally, are you ready for Thursday's exam?" Sally: "We'll see if grandpa pulls through," etc. After seemingly everyone in her classes this semester had lost at least one grandparent during the term, Nicole Gardner, second year graduate student and composition instructor, swore that with the next one she would ask for a copy of the death certificate. "Well, here's a new one," she said after she read Chelsea's e-mail, and she went back to her own work without responding. *Let her sweat it out*, she decided.

chapter twenty-one

sock hops, not much

'Round eleven Chelsea called Po. He had wondered if she would call, and as it got later and later he was beginning to doubt and reassess, wondering if the earlier conversation had been even worse than he had first thought. Tired of obsessing about it, he put on PBS and started nodding off. Just as he was drifting off to sleepy land, he heard the phone.

"Hi," she said.

"Hey, Chelsea, um, Hi."

"I hope it's not too late. I thought I'd call to say goodnight."

"No," he said groggily as came to his senses, dug the remote from out of the cushion, and flicked off the TV. "I was just hanging out. Apparently watching Masterpiece Theater."

"I see. Is it a masterpiece?"

"The usual costume-drama thing, English people out on a lawn, some love triangle or rhombus, I'd say. They decided Piece of Crap Theater wasn't the best title, I think. No car chases yet."

"Or carriage chases?"

"Or flying knickers. How's your paper coming along?"

"I'm getting there."

"Have you saved the world?"

"Oh, probably."

"Nice. So, you'll be happy, I've thought of an excellent date for us tomorrow night."

"Yay! I can't wait. Is it a masterpiece? What's the exciting plan?"

"It's a surprise."

"Aw, now you're just teasing me."

"I can probably get out of the office by 6. Want to meet at 7:30 or 8? I'll pick you up."

"Perfect! I wish my time machine were ready, I'd skip right to then, make this paper disappear!"

"That's what you get for buying an American model, I suppose."

"Yes, the Slovaks make the best ones."

"And the Magyars."

"Hee-hee. Where do they live?"

"Magyaria?"

"Madagascar maybe?"

"They live somewhere, I know that, with excellent time machines. 100,000 year warranties standard."

"Don't pooh-pooh the Slovaks."

"I never would. My flying saucer is from Slovakia."

"Uh-huh. You only have one?"

"It's a deluxe model. More like a battle cruiser, really."

"Not bad."

"What do you have, a fleet?"

"That's right."

"Where do you keep them all?"

"Some in the future, some in the past, hence the need for the – "

"Time machine, aha, I got it. The answer to America's storage problems once and for all!"

"*Word.*"

"Word?" Po couldn't help but chuckle. Chelsea was quivering with pent up laughter and trying not to lose it, "to lose her shit," as she would say. She could imagine them joking around like this every night in bed, with tickling and the works.

"Word, that's right, you heard me."

"I can't argue with that. What's the best comeback?"

"*Words.* Duh."

"But then we would be having words, which is like a fight, isn't it? Hey, do you ever use the expression, 'May I have a word'? One of the Brits just used it on the tube."

"I just said 'May I have a word' today, actually."

"Really?"

"Oh yes, to a dictionary salesman." She could barely get the sentence out, her face hurt so much from holding back the laughs. Corny gold.

"Ha. I didn't realize they sold them by the slice."

"By the syllable, on the installment plan."

"Ugh! Okay, cutie, you're getting giddy. I need to crash and you need to write."

"Boo. All right, I'll say goodnight then. I'll see you soon — in the future."

"Very soon."

""Goodnight, Po." Then after she hung up and put the phone down, she couldn't help herself and closed her eyes dreamily and said, "I love you."

♪ ♪ ♪

Chelsea lucubrated until very late (hey, if you don't know what "lucubrate" means, look it up) but managed to finish her paper before passing out. She caught the bus in the morning and made it to class on time with the final draft ready — many of her classmates weren't so punctual or diligent. With still a few minutes before the teacher would arrive, she and Carrie chatted.

"Hey sister, whatcha been up to?" Carrie asked, with a hint of forlornness or some less awkward phrase.

"Not much." Chelsea couldn't help but smile and glow.

"Not much, eh? Not much 'win the lottery' or not much as in 'I just wrote an A paper'?

"Hee-hee. Not much 'I met someone.'"

"Ooh, right on! Who is the lucky boy?"

"Not a boy."

"A chick? Hmm . . . now that is interesting," she said with more hushed tones, scooting her chair closer. "I guess we've all dabbled."

"No," Chelsea laughed, "I mean a *man*."

"A man? As in over 25?"

Chelsea nodded.

"How about that! I guess our talk about that gave you some ideas. Sexy ideas, ooh la la. Who is he? A grad student?" Chelsea shook her head no.

Carrie's eyes widened. "Don't tell me a prof!"

"No, no. He's in the real world — a legal investigator, clerk, studying for the bar."

"Man! Someone in this town that old who isn't part of

the college, on parole, or a meth junkie? I'll be damned."

"He's really smart, funny . . . "

"Not a Christian?"

"*Definitely* not a Christian."

"Maybe he has a very personal relationship with Jesus."

"No way."

"Wow, you did hit the 'not much' jackpot. That's great!" Carrie was delighted for her friend but more than a little envious, given the parade of losers she'd saddled herself with over the last few years.

"You'll like him, Carrie."

Just then Ms. Gardner entered. "Oh wait, here comes the bitch," Carrie said, louder than you'd think; her classmates had come to expect this tone from her, so hardly an eyebrow raised. "I want all the details later. All the dirt. Every goddamn thing."

♪ ♪ ♪

Chelsea gave Carrie a sketch of the romantic developments over lunch, not wanting to say too much and possibly jinx things. Carrie wondered what the hell Chelsea was doing visiting a retirement home in the first place, to meet the woman that would put her in her will and cause Po to come a-knockin'. "Be careful, such altruism and fortuitousness could

162

easily lead to religiousness," she warned her. "Remember, it's just chance, not some stupid miracle. Don't make me have to come to one of these old folks homes to kick your ass." Chelsea assured her it was only for the money.

"Swear to God?" Carrie asked with a wink, and Chelsea crossed her heart. "Well, all right then," Carrie said as they were parting. "I'd suggest a double-date, but I probably should keep Fido away from the public at large." Fido was a reference to Franz, her current Euro-trash tattoo-ridden punk rocker drug addict boyfriend — not the first and not the last. It would be a long time before Carrie would start to see the pattern, though, and even longer before she would break the man-mold. Chelsea, meanwhile, survived her two afternoon classes then danced through the rest of the day, eagerly awaiting Po's surprise date.

♪ ♪ ♪

Word was spreading fast about Gerald's demise at the local high school, typically in the following fashion:

Student A: Hey, did you hear that Gerald Edwards died?

Student B: Who?

Student A: Some geeky kid. A sophomore. Played the accordion.

Student B: Oh yeah. He died?

163

Student A: Yeah, supposedly he ate the Five Alarm Habanero Death Chili at Boles and flames shot out his ass and he died.

Student B: No kidding!

Student A: It set his internal organs on fire.

Student B: Really?

Student A: Something like that.

Student B: Wow. What did he look like?

Student A: Greasy hair, I think. Zits. Hyper laugh. That's what somebody told me.

Student B: Oh yeah. Didn't you used to beat up that kid?

Student A: Probably. You can't expect me to remember all of them.

Most of the core information remained the same, although there would be alterations to step 3, such as "Yeah, he ate the Six Alarm Habanero Death Chili at Boles and a pepper jammed sideways in his throat and he died," or "Yeah, he ate the Twelve Alarm Jalapeño Death Chili at Boles and his face incinerated," or "Yeah, he ate the Eight Alarm Ancho Death Chili at Boles and his stomach exploded," or "Yeah, he ate the Nine Alarm Habanero Death Chili at Boles and died of heat stroke," or "He was raped by a badger and died," but everyone, even the Special Ed students, by late morning got the idea that someone had died, that is, except for those who stayed home sick that day (although many of the latter received text messages from their friends and found out anyway). At 1:30, the principal, Mr. Holling, came on the PA system to make an announcement:

"Teachers, students, employees, and friends: It is with deep sadness and a very heavy heart that I must announce the passing of one of our own, Edward, er, ahem, excuse me, Gerald Edwards, who died in an unfortunate accident on Saturday. Gerald loved music, laughter, long distance running, and calculus. On behalf of the school, I would like to sent out our sincere condolences to his family and friends . . ." — at this point all the students in each of the classrooms looked at each other in askance, curious as to who these friends might exactly be, but the result was only confused faces and shoulder shrugs — "Let us pause in remembrance, a moment of silence."

And so it was. Holling waited a solid thirty seconds and then continued: "God keep us all. Exams will be canceled for the remainder of the week." At this last part a collective cheer let out that could be heard across the street, which muffled out Holling's parting "Thank you." A few of the teachers audibly groaned, wondering how this postponement would affect their already tight schedules for the remainder of the term. Most, however, had long stopped caring about anything.

Needless to say, the overwhelming majority of the kids,

these shining young pearls of humanity, were ecstatic with the reprieve. Many were already planning to break out the black armbands for Tuesday, a fitting tribute to a fallen, semi-anonymous comrade who had given them so much more in death than in life. One student even remarked, "I'm glad he didn't die during summer vacation!"

At 6:15 pm, intentionally during the nightly news so that it might be broadcast live — which the one local television station did do — Boles held a press conference from the restaurant, first reading a prepared statement, with his typical melodramatic flourishes:

"Hello everyone, I am here today to express my personal regret and sympathies over a sad occurrence at Boles' restaurant this past weekend, one that led to the untimely death of a fine member of our community, Gerald Edwards. By all accounts, he was a wonderful young man with tremendous promise. I understand he wanted to be the first person to play the accordion in outer space. I went to school with his mother, Gladys, and I am broken-hearted at her loss. The Chinese have a saying, and I paraphrase, 'son bury parents, all is right with the world, but parents bury son, all is wrong.' Things are not right in our world, my friends, not right at all, when a mother and father must say such a goodbye to a fifteen-year-old son. But I want to assure you all that our food here is safe, our legendary

166

chili is safe, the same now as it has always been. This was an isolated incident, a freak occurrence. We all need to grieve and mourn, true, but after that, we need to be strong for Gerald and move forward with our lives and dining, as I'm sure he would have wanted."

Boles then fielded questions from the three reporters in attendance. The first few of the queries had to do with the secret ingredient, whether it was gasoline or rat poison, and Boles dodged these queries repeatedly and effectively as if he were a seasoned politician. He even imagined this all being a stepping-stone to a successful mayoral campaign. He did love the spotlight so . . . and often pictured himself as Marilyn Monroe singing happy birthday to JFK, curling his shoulders, etc. Frankly, Boles was aggrieved more by the low turnout for the press conference than by the death of his former classmate's son. Claude Boles, the already bi-curious theater type (or, as he preferred to spell it, *theatre*) in high school just as he was now, barely knew the snooty girly-girl Gladys, to be honest—he was in a very different social circle, a different universe.

Under his dark gray suit Boles was wearing . . . bicycle shorts.

One of the reporters raised his hand to ask a final question.

"Yes, Bob?" Boles said as he sipped from a water bottle.

167

"It's Jim, actually, from the Times-Telegram. Jim Myers. I live across the street from you, remember? Mr. Boles, in light of what has happened, are there plans to rename the chili?"

"Well, I have given some thought to this. There are no official plans as such at this juncture, but we will certainly consider that option. If that family deems it is appropriate, I think it would be a fitting tribute to rename it the 'Gerald Edwards Memorial Five Alarm Habanero Eternal Life Chili.'"

Po watched this surreal exchange at home on the television as he was just getting home from work and sifting through the junk mail. "Hmm," he said, without giving it much thought. He had his eyes on a bigger prize tonight . . . his sheets were still clean, he determined, and he checked his condom supply, again "just in case." "This could be true love," he thought to himself, "but it most definitely could be sex." In this world of ours the two are not so easily distinguished. He would even scrub and trim his woolly mane of pubic hair "just in case," and the nether region south of his scrotum, wondering if Chelsea's nose might cheerfully end up somewhere in that general vicinity in a few hours.

Chelsea had similar thoughts and spent extra time shaving her legs and cooch. She decided to wear a green paisley summer dress (even though it was an unseasonably cold spring day, it was her favorite article of clothing) and her lucky blue cardigan sweater, plus black Doc Marten boots. Her mother said she looked lovely, like the sun shining on a meadow, that the dress made the green and blue in Chelsea's eyes sparkle like the ocean, which was good enough for Chelsea.

Po arrived at 7:45, and both mother and daughter could hardly contain their excitement. He kissed Chelsea's cheek and handed her a violet that he had concealed behind his back.

"Hi," he said.

"Hi yourself," Chelsea replied sweetly.

"And hello, Mrs. Walker."

"Please, Po, *Ellen*."

"Sorry, this politeness of mine is a terrible habit."

"Yes, you'd better watch it or you'll get one hell of a hug! So did Chelsea mention that we'd like to invite you to a nice home-cooked meal this week?"

"She did. I'd love to."

"Great! She and I are quite the team. How about Wednesday night?"

Po looked at Chelsea for confirmation. "Fine by me," she said.

"Wednesday, that sounds perfect."

"All right, I'll leave you two kids be. Take good care of my little girl, Po."

"Mom!" Chelsea blushed, as her mother kissed her

forehead.

"Have fun!" She left the room.

"So what's the plan, Paprika?"

"Oh, that again!" Po did like this pet name. His last girlfriend had called him "Pootie." "Phase one is at my place, if that's okay."

"Of course. I can't wait!" Chelsea was wondering exactly how far she should go with an older man for whom she already had such strong feelings, but she had concluded long before that she would feel things out, trust her instincts, and if one thing led to another and felt right, so be it. Po reached down, held her hand, and the two walked out of the house toward his car. He unlocked the door for her and whispered in her ear, "You look beautiful." She felt a jolt of electricity and magic surge through her body.

"Thank you."

"I like the paisleys. Everything." He walked around the sedan to the driver's side and got in. Prominent in the well dash, which Chelsea immediately noticed, was a miniature alligator fashioned from a macadamia nut, some sort of Native American artwork.

"How are you? You turned in your paper?" Po asked as he started the engine.

"Uh-huh. An instant American classic."

"Nice. So the cheeseburger of essays."

"With ketchup. How was your day?"

"Other than being bombarded by trillions and trillions of neutrinos against my will, I can't complain."

"Ah, you need a titanium-thread cardigan, like mine. It is neutrino-resistant and deflects most of your subatomic particles." She struck a pose in her seat.

"I was thinking of buying one. Where'd you get it?"

"Oh, I know people."

He looked over at her and smiled. "People? What sort of people?"

She put her finger on the side of her nose. "People who are in the know, if you know what I mean. People worth knowing."

"The sweater people."

"That's right."

"Hey, did you catch that news conference from Boles'?"

"No, what? When?" Chelsea suddenly felt a cold splash of reality before remembering to feign nonchalance.

"It was on during the news, just before I left home."

"What was it about?"

"Oh, about your friend . . ."

Acquaintance, Chelsea thought angrily, but did not say it.

"Your friend, Gerald, right? Mostly just condolence

171

stuff. Nothing all that interesting. The reporters were pressing the owner—Mr. Boles, right?—for the secret ingredient, wondering if that's what killed the boy. No real information. It's funny what passes for news out here."

Chelsea was silent. Po noticed and again looked away from the road at Chelsea.

"I'm sorry. I didn't mean 'funny.' You know what I mean." He reached over and squeezed her hand. She smiled lovingly at him and squeezed back.

"It's okay. No big deal."

"Do you want to talk about it?"

"No, not tonight. Let's just enjoy ourselves! Yay! Surprise date night!"

"We're here," Po pointed out as he pulled into the lot for his condo complex.

"That was quick."

"Yup. It's only a mile or two." He stepped out of the car, and she let herself before he could open the door for her. They walked up to his condo, which was a second floor unit, holding hands. "Well, this is it."

"Yay," she said eagerly. He unlocked the door to reveal a handsomely decorated place, with earth tones, touches of olive green throughout, including the sofa, settee, and matching chair, tasteful art with exotic themes—but everything was sort of

172

standard and spoke to youthful yuppieness, nothing daring or all that distinct, no real personality. There were a few houseplants, all of which seemed overly trimmed and controlled. A table was set for two, with long lavender (unlit for now) candles.

"So dinner is the surprise?"

"After the surprise. Would you like a tour?"

"I would love one." It is customary the first time that humans walk into each other's living quarters to give a cursory tour. Po successfully made light of the absurdity of it all while at the same time being proud of his place. "Well, welcome to the domicile. As you can see, this is the living room directly in front of you."

"Nice fireplace."

"Thank you. It's for burning wood and . . . " he tried to think of a clever joke. "Uh, evidence."

"That's what they are for. I like the sofa, the warm colors."

"You can't spell furniture without 'fun,' you know," he said cheekily.

"You also can't spell it without 'urine,'" she pointed out.

He thought about this, couldn't help but picture her squatting over his sitting chair urinating, and shuddered a bit. "You're right. But I guess that is fun for some people."

"Just another Saturday night for some."

"Good thing it's Monday."

"Ha. Next stop?"

He took her hand and led her around to the kitchen, which was small but with impressive natural light. "This is what some call a 'kitchen.'"

"*Kit-chen?*" She played along, pronouncing the word slowly as if hearing a foreign language.

"Yes. This is where foo-foo is prepared and stored. The drawers and cupboards contain food implements and food stuffs."

"Ah. *Foo foo.*"

Then they quickly peeked into the bathroom, and then went around the corner into the ever-mysterious, imposing bedroom, and stood before his large bed. "And what do you call this?" she inquired.

"This, my dear, is the bedroom. It's for sleeping and fort-building."

"Forts I know, but *slee-ping?*"

"Yes, think of it as dream cultivation. The bedroom is a greenhouse for dreams."

"Aha. That side job of yours. A gardener."

"This could also be the venue for spooning." He said enticingly.

174

She smiled. "I've heard of this." He led her back to the main room, while she wondered how many girls had received this tour.

"And now for the surprise. Okay, sit down on the sofa and close your eyes."

"Okay." She did as ordered, putty in his hands.

"Don't open them until I say when." He sat down beside her, reached down under the couch and grabbed a pair of white tube socks. "All right, *when*."

Sill smiling, she opened her eyes to see the gym socks.

"Uh?"

"Chelsea, you have been cordially invited to a '50s style sock hop!"

"A sock hop!"

"That's right." He laid the socks down on the floor in front of them. "Now let's make those socks hop," and he leaned over and kissed her passionately.

"I love socks," she whispered, her face flush. "I think they hopped."

"Oh yes," and he kissed her again.

After the long kiss, she caught her breath. "Sock hops are the best."

"There's more."

"Oh?"

Po got up, went into the other room and returned with a shoebox, and happily sat beside her again. "In this box is all we need to make . . . sock puppets!!!"

To Chelsea, it was like a dream come true. She put her hand over her mouth as if to stop the smile from escaping into orbit. "I *love* sock puppets!"

"I somehow knew you would."

The shoebox contained sharpies, yarn, needle and thread, buttons, assorted bric-a-brac, including all kinds of little fuzzy things that Chelsea adored.

"Where did you get all this wonderful stuff?"

"Oh, I've been saving up for a rainy day, or a special someone," he said softly, warmly.

And so they played and the time danced along. They listened to music, mostly goofy '50s and '60s pop songs that he had slapped on a CD for the occasion. She made a sock puppet that looked like Jesus, although she referred to it as a "random hippie," and he constructed one of Eleanor Roosevelt crossed with a space alien. Then they wore each other's sock puppets and improvised a play that ended with the two characters making out, the two puppeteers in a giggle fit and then emulating the puppets. One thing led to another and let's just say that some random hippie or space alien peering through the balcony window would have seen some interesting inter-

176

personal contortions and sexy gymnastics on Po's living room floor. Po rather effectively put a sock in it, *it* being what Henry Miller would call a valise.

After the love wrasslin', with other appetites now aroused, Po, lighter by a few ounces, then scrounged around his take-out menu pile, standing in his boxer-briefs. *Chinese? Mexican? Pizza?* The two decided on Thai. Chelsea, red-faced in post-orgasmic glow, chose Sweet 'n' Sour fried tofu and vegetables (she was getting much closer to being a vegetarian), while Po went for the standard Chicken Pad Thai. Chelsea lay on the floor, her face against Po's discarded shirt, and breathed in the scene, her senses heightened while her internal organs shifted back into place. This blissful contentment was irreversibly tainted by Po's unadventurous and rather mundane food choice, however; she instantly realized that she would remember what he ordered and all that it said about his personality even more vividly than she would remember the way the sex felt—as if the pad thai weighed more than his body on hers.

She closed her eyes and tried to think it away but knew it was too late. *Damn time machine in the shop!* she thought and smiled, just as he laid back down next to her. He kissed the itchy bumps left on her shoulder from the carpet, and she ran her fingers along the scratches she had made on his back. She tried to convince herself that he was not as ordinary as he was beginning to seem. Remember the sock puppets. Maybe he was thinking the same thing about her. Maybe we should just accept that we are all ordinary. Still, deep inside she knew that she wanted more, just like she felt with Darren. She wanted . . . greatness. It felt good but she hoped she might—no, she expected—that she would levitate. How does the song go, "is that all there is?" The response is "let's keep dancing/Let's break out the booze and have a ball." Maybe a good time and "good enough" is all there is, so she watched him eat his pad thai then fucked him some more.

Around 2 am, he asked her if she wanted to sleep over, and a bit offended that he even would ask without assuming she would, she said she had an early class tomorrow and needed to go home.

"Are you sure?"

"Yes, I'm sorry."

"Okay, I'll take you."

Back in his car, they held hands, but it didn't feel quite right to her. "Can I ask you something?" She said.

"Of course, anything."

"If we had ordered pizza, what kind would you have wanted?"

"I don't know, pepperoni or cheese probably You?"

Chelsea decided it was best to lie. "The same." Could she truly love a man who didn't say artichoke hearts or spinach or eggplant or something deliciously freaky? "Hey, tell me something, Po—if you had a dog, what would name it?"

"A dog? Why would I have a dog?"

This was getting worse and worse. "Just 'what if.'"

"Hmm . . . Maybe Rover? Spot?"

"Even if he didn't have spots?" Chelsea felt some hope.

"Well, that would be strange. What would you name your dog?"

"Proton." Or her first-born son, whichever came first.

"Really? That's hilarious." Po glanced away from the road, looked at her and smiled. Chelsea was disappointed, basically heartbroken, that he would even doubt her seriousness for a second. Still, she would have to think about all of this. Was it his fault he had such normal tendencies? Wasn't he trying to be more?

chapter twenty-two

squirrelgate

"Misgivings" is an interesting word, suggesting more than just doubt or unease, but also that which has been given poorly, improperly, or dysfunctionally, met with regret on the part of the giver. What Chelsea had given to Po could not ever be completely restored to her. To offer love and to receive sex in return is kind of a strange exchange that never quite feels right. Love seems to float between the physical and spiritual, the mundane and sublime; Plato imagined it being a bridge, but maybe nothing can span the gulf. On Tuesday Chelsea benefited from some time apart from Po to fend off the majority of her misgivings, reconstructing him fairly well in her mind as "the One." He clearly was more of the One than anyone else she had been with. Absence may not necessarily make the heart grow fonder, but it does seem to make it easier to do its thing—or better said, the mind, which is where 95% of romance occurs and probably where the "heart" as the wellspring of emotions is actually located. Do we love the Other as much as our own fantasies and projections? Having the lover around constantly can only lead to disappointments, a fallen idol. A skilled suitor knows this and will manage the necessary spaces effectively. It is true that sheer over-saturation will create a certain addiction and dependence, but that isn't love, whatever love is.

With Chelsea's scent still on his lips and fingertips, Po wrote her an e-mail once he settled in at work. Staring at the computer screen, he replayed images in his head from the night before, admiring his own handiwork as well as his solid sexual performance. "Not bad for such a drought! Sock puppets, ha!"

> *Dear Chelsea,*
>
> *You were so beautiful last night. I would travel in a time machine with you anywhere, anytime. Thank you for being you. See you at your place for dinner tomorrow?*

And then he wondered whether to sign it *with love* or not. After having made love, it would be very evident if he didn't write it, but did he want to give the impression of such seriousness? Wasn't he serious? He could picture himself boning this girl for a long while, he thought to himself in those exact crude words. Was he "head over heels," as we say? What an odd expression, as if falling in love is like falling off a bicycle. He remembered as a ten year-old riding his bike down a hill, hitting an exposed tree root and completely wiping out. If he hadn't turned his flying body at the last instant, he would have landed right on his head instead of his shoulder. He dislocated it severely and it gave him problems for years. Now he couldn't even recall whether it was his left or right. He sat in his desk chair and squeezed one and then the other with the opposite hand as he looked at the letter he was about to send. An alternative would be to be humorous and sign the letter "ga-ga," as in "ga ga over you," but again, while sillier, it still seemed overly serious. He decided to go with "love and sock puppets," hoping to tap into the sense of fun that had preceded and inspired the balling.

Chelsea waited until late afternoon to write back, and she even considered not answering at all, just for the hell of it. The idea was entirely hers, not Darlene's. Darlene hadn't been around for a while, likely out of protest of the entire romance. Chelsea responded to Po's e-mail, but subconsciously included some rather unsettling undertones. If Po were more attentive he might have noticed the subtle but distinct change in feel, how Chelsea's love was become more restrained and she was beginning to erect defenses.

> Dear Po,
>
> Thank you. So we will see you for dinner tomorrow at 7 pm? My mother will be excited, especially when she watches me kiss you at the table and transcend time. Say hello to your sock puppet for me.
>
> Love,
> Chelsea

Wednesday arrived. Po this time brought a bottle of wine along with flowers for both Chelsea and her mother. *Flowers again,* Chelsea said to herself as she invited him in. *What am I, a racehorse who has delivered a victory?* Chelsea's mother was elated. Mother and daughter had collaborated on two impressive lasagnas, one with red sauce and the other white, and a lovely spinach salad. This was complemented by a fresh store-bought baguette, with a homemade chocolate cream pie for dessert. It was a fine dinner. Chelsea's mother mostly quizzed Po on his law school experience. Chelsea for her part engaged in the charming banter Po had come to expect, but it felt a bit like acting. Her heart wasn't really in it.

After the main course, Po leaned back, sated and happy.

"So tell me, Ellen, do you two cook together often?"

"Oh, on special occasions. Usually it's just Chelsea, me, and her Aunt Amy together on holidays, so we'll all tinker around together in the kitchen."

"This was wonderful."

"Thank you."

"Are you and Amy close, Chelsea?"

Chelsea wasn't entirely there, so she was somewhat startled to be addressed.

"Huh? Oh, yes, she's a riot."

Chelsea's mother stood up and began to clear the dishes. "She's my sister and I love her, but she's also a foul-mouthed cynic."

"Who can blame her?" Chelsea asked defensively.

"You'd be surprised how much energy a little sunshine can create."

"What does that mean?" While she tried to make it seem like she was joking, Chelsea was being unmistakably peevish. Even Po picked up on this.

"It means *smile*, be warm, radiate."

"Oh please, Mom."

"Wait right there, you two, there's still dessert. Chocolate pie!"

"All right," Po said loudly, for Ellen's benefit.   He

reached over and gave Chelsea a peck on the cheek. "Hi."

"Hi." She cracked a tiny smile.

"Everything okay?"

"Sure. I think I'm just a little on edge. School and everything."

"And your friend, too, I suppose."

"Friend?"

"You know, Gerald, right?"

"Oh, yes, exactly." Just then the phone rang. Mrs. Walker picked it up in the kitchen, after peeking her head in from the other room and announcing, "I'm sorry, I should get that. Please excuse me, Po"

While the mother talked, Po said to Chelsea, "Your mother is so nice."

"She is."

"Do you get it from her or does she get it from you?"

"From me. Time machine, remember."

"Ha."

"It's cool that you cook together. Did she help you with your science fair projects when you were a kid, too?"

Chelsea didn't think this was humorous. "Nope, they were all mine."

"What were some that you did?"

"Well, since you ask, I had these friends that were twins,

and one year I compared the effects of various kinds of products on them, one brand versus another, that kind of thing."

"Like what?"

"Oh, like which kinds of hairspray irritated their eyes the most, and which dish soap tasted the worst." Chelsea laughed at her own evil.

"You sprayed them in the eyes with hairspray?" Po couldn't tell whether she was being honest or not or concocting one of their already-familiar comic exchanges.

"Sure. No joke."

"What grade did you get?"

"I think a B. The teacher said the experiments were well-constructed and reported but made some comment about a Nazi doctor."

"Josef Mengele?"

"That sounds right. I didn't quite follow what she was getting at."

Chelsea's mother came back into the room with the dessert plates and forks. "Now that was an odd call."

"Who was it?" Po asked.

"Jan Edwards, Gerald's mom."

"Gerald the one who just, um, passed away?"

"That's right. The Medical Examiner called her today and confirmed that Gerald had peanuts in his system. Gerald was deathly allergic of nuts. Somehow there were nuts in the chili. They think it might have something to do with the secret ingredient, which turned out to be squirrel meat, of all things!"

"Peanuts?" Po instantly replayed in his mind the scene in the orchestra hall, with Chelsea and the bag of nuts, the *bag,* the *nuts,* the connection was made. He couldn't help but to wonder, *did she? Could she? No way, it doesn't make sense.* He went visibly pale. Chelsea lowered her head and looked down at her plate.

"That's right. And squirrel! Whoever heard of such a chili? When everyone finds out about this, it will be a scandal. That Boles has some explaining to do. What do you think about that, Chelsea?"

"Beats me, I had the soup. Squirrel, really?"

"So it wasn't the peppers at all, they said. Did you know Gerry was allergic to peanuts?"

"I don't remember it. Was he?"

"That reminds me, Jan mentioned that the funeral service will be Friday morning, at the high school auditorium, and that she would like you to play, if you're still willing. Twice your normal fee. I told her of course you would do it for free, since Gerald was such a good friend." Chelsea's eyebrows raised indicating slight disgust that she quickly concealed. Her mother continued: "She'll call tomorrow with all the specifics.

She's trying to be strong, God bless her. Oh, I should go get the pie. Wait one sec!"

Po and Chelsea sat in silence. Ellen returned almost instantly. "When I was a little girl, I don't recall anyone being allergic to nuts, or milk, or wheat, and now it seems these kids are allergic to everything. I wonder why. Po, do you have any allergies like that?"

"No, I don't. Not in my family at all. Hardy Russian stock, I guess."

"Chelsea's allergic to aloe, that's it."

"Mom, please."

"What? It's true. Aren't we among friends?" She gave her daughter a wink.

"Aloe, that's interesting, since it's supposed to soothe," Po said distractedly.

"It gives me a rash and makes my skin sag," Chelsea added.

"They put it in all those skin creams, right?"

"It's everywhere," Mrs. Walker chimed in. "Sunscreen, shaving cream, bath oil."

"Everything except soup and chili, I guess," Po couldn't help but say, which was followed by a very awkward silence.

"Well, I should serve up this pie. What size piece, Po?"

"Oh, um, ample."

"This big?" Ellen carved him a solid quarter of the pie.

"Give me a slab, ha."

After dessert they all had coffee and chatted a bit more, then Po apologized but said he needed to get home, that he had an early morning to help one of the partners with court the next day. Chelsea walked him out onto the landing, wondering why he hadn't mentioned before that he would have to leave so early. She sensed his suspicions, of course. He was avoiding looking her in the eyes.

"Peanuts, huh?"

"That is strange, isn't it," Chelsea replied.

"Filberts maybe?" he laughed nervously. "Well, I really should go, sweet pea." He leaned in and kissed her on the lips, but it was an abbreviated kiss, like he was kissing a stranger. She noticed this.

"Bye, Po. Sleep well. Call me tomorrow?"

"I will. Bye."

♪ ♪ ♪

Chelsea went back into the house. Her mother was in the kitchen washing dishes. Chelsea came in and without a word, started putting the dried dishes away.

"Are you okay, honey?" Her mother asked with

intuitive maternal concern.

"Uh-huh."

"Hmm. Everything fine with Po?"

"I suppose."

"Are you sure?"

"Mom, can I ask you something?"

"Of course, anything."

"How do you know if a person is 'the One'? I mean, what was it like for you and Dad?"

Mrs. Walker put down the dish she was rinsing and turned toward her daughter. "Well . . . I'm not sure if he was."

"Really?" Chelsea was truly surprised.

"Make no mistake, Chelsea, your father was a beautiful man. He could turn my knees to jelly. The first time we kissed, I saw fireworks and lightning, just like in the movies. But . . ." she paused.

"But?"

"But I always had my doubts. Some nights he'd be asleep, and I would lay there next to him and think maybe he wasn't who I thought he was, or that I wasn't who he thought, that we were strangers who had just been swept up in this life, that it was all a . . ."

"A lie?"

"Well, more like a play, like we were just playing parts.

Especially after he died, I wondered if I had always been meant to be with someone else, and I missed that person by being with your father."

A stunned Chelsea stood in silence and could only say, "Wow."

"Brains are busy things, sweetheart. Minds wander. It's only natural. You're having doubts about Po?"

"I guess."

"I think he's a nice young man. If you're wondering about whether to take the next step—I know you're a woman now and the way things are—you just need to trust your judgment, and be safe."

Chelsea averted her eyes, thought about telling her that the cows were already out of the barn, a suitably goofy expression that her mother would understand. The socks had already hopped. "Uh . . ."

"Yes, honey?"

"Uh, thanks, Mom."

"Aww, give me a hug. Everything will be all right. Follow your heart. There'll be plenty of time to be rational and sensible when you're older." The two embraced, and Chelsea thought that this was the best advice her mother had ever given her.

Chelsea went in to go to bed, and Darlene had quite

191

different advice. She appeared on Chelsea's night stand, angrily waiting, tapping her feet, her arms folded.

"He knows."

"I know."

"He knows!" Darlene screamed.

"I said I know, what do you want me to do?"

"He's the only one who can connect you to the peanuts. You have to take care of him."

"What? Ship him?"

"Yes! A-S-A-P."

"That's your answer to everything. No, I will not. I love him."

"Oh please, you do not."

"Maybe I do."

"You don't."

"I could."

"Yeah, pepperoni pizza?"

Chelsea dejectedly sat on the bed. Darlene had won the argument. "What should I do?"

"We'll think of something."

♪ ♪ ♪

That following morning it was absolute chaos at Boles'.

Apparently some reporters had come in from the nearby towns and cities, as there were now ten to fifteen members of the media clamoring about in front of the restaurant when the staff arrived to open for breakfast. Word had leaked about the squirrel meat and nuts. The assistant manager called Boles, who got a barebones briefing, enough to say "Holy Shit!" He peeled off his bicycle shorts, took a frantic shower, and rushed downtown as fast as he could to face the press, in his haste forgetting to brush his teeth or apply deodorant. His dreams of being mayor were evaporating faster than eyeball juice in Death Valley.

"Yes, we admit that the 'secret' ingredient in the Five Alarm Habanero Death Chili" — it was telling that, now cornered, he used *we* instead of *I* — "is game meat. No, it is not always squirrel. It depends on what the chef happens to catch in his backyard. We can assure you that the animals are taken humanely, checked for diseases, and cleaned properly." *Taken* is the hunter's euphemism for killed/slaughtered.

"And what about the nuts?" inquired Jim Myers from the *Times-Telegraph*.

"Yes, well," Boles stammered as he wiped his brow. "In the course of preparation it can happen that certain counter scraps might find their way into dish. We're not sure how the nuts gravitated to that part of the kitchen, but cooking is not a scientific process, it is an art, an impressionistic process, like

193

Monet or Degas or . . ."

"Van Gogh?"

"That's right, Van Gogh, and look at how much his paintings are worth."

"Are you comparing your chili to a Van Gogh? Did he paint with squirrel meat?" asked another reporter, one who wasn't at the first press conference. Everyone laughed heartily, however inappropriately, but Boles, of course.

"We have no further comment about that. Next?"

"Do you anticipate a law suit from the family, or perhaps criminal charges?"

"I have left messages with Jan Edwards and her husband again expressing my profound regret" — it was now back to *I* — "but as of yet I have not heard back from the family. I personally have a meeting scheduled with local authorities later today, purely informational, from what I understand. There is an ongoing investigation. We're sure the authorities will be satisfied that there was no criminal wrongdoing or negligence in this matter."

"And the Board of Health? What has it said about your squirrelly chili?"

"No comment. Thank you for your time." With that Boles curtly ended the Q&A, went to the back room, closed the door, and dug around in his desk for an aspirin. Finding only a flask of bourbon, he took a good long stiff drink and thought about those movies where embattled characters stick a gun in their mouths and *blammo*. There is surely something homoerotic about a pistol in the mouth instead of the more intellectual gun to the temple, so it is no surprise that Boles, given his history, would consider it the preferred suicide option. He would tough it out, but what would become known in the town as "squirrelgate" — and permanently solidify Boles' reputation as a dangerous buffoon — had begun. "A beautiful political career nipped in the bud by a lousy rodent, damn it all to hell," Boles said to the bourbon, still deluding himself. *Squirrels were rodents, right?* He then smelled his armpit and made a yucky face, realizing at that moment he had forgotten the Right Guard.

chapter twenty-three
descartes

Chelsea sat by the same fountain where she and Po first kissed, deep in thought. She had zoned out on the bus ride that morning, missed her bus stop and had to walk from the other end of campus. Now she decided to sit here and meditate instead of attending her first class. Meditation ideally involves clearing the head of any thoughts, unperturbed by the word. Taoists speak of being like an uncarved block, *pu,* which is a funny word for it. Chelsea watched sorority whores stroll by caked in make-up and for the first time truly wondered if she was any better than them. Her sense of superiority and condescension had been an unwavering source of strength and conviction for most of her life. *What really does separate us from each other?* Does anything matter? She then heard a familiar voice calling her.

"Hey, fiddler!"

"Farza!" Chelsea couldn't remember ever being so glad to see her imaginary acquaintance. He came up on his scooter and plopped himself down beside her. She had missed his brightness.

"Where have you been all my life, sweet cheeks?"

"I could ask the same of you."

"Busy, busy. That visit to the psychic really got me thinking."

"It did? You didn't even talk to her."

"I know. That's it. I started thinking, maybe there is this amazing future waiting for me, but I've been to scared to find out about it for myself, to make the leap, to face the music."

"I know what you mean."

"So I've decided to join the Peace Corps."

"What? The Peace Corps?"

"That's right."

"So you're leaving?"

"In two weeks. They're sending me to Africa. Senegal."

"Africa? The Peace Corps?" Chelsea's head was spinning. "Farza . . ."

"What?"

"You do know that you are imaginary, don't you?"

197

Chelsea hadn't crossed this particular line with him in a long time.

"What, and the Peace Corps isn't? You aren't? Have you taken a real look at yourself lately?"

"I-" Chelsea had no answer.

"It'll be good for me. Don't worry. I'm probably not in a high risk group to get AIDS, ha."

"That's not funny. I'm going to worry about you. And Africa is a fucked-up place."

"Oh, come on, we've known each other a long time, we've done some fun stuff together, but, let's be honest, we're not all that close. At some point we all need to grow up."

"What about Carrie? You still like her, don't you?"

"She doesn't even know I'm alive. Maybe when I come back she'll take notice, something might have changed, but I'm not going to hold my breath."

"When will you be back?"

"Three years, at most four."

"Oh." Chelsea was suddenly very sad and felt abandoned, betrayed.

"It's nothing. You have three more years of college, I have three years in Senegal. Turn that frown upside down or sideways or whatever, Chelsea. You should be happy for me. I'm maturing . . . I think."

"I guess. It seems like you're running away, though. And I need you."

"Nah, you don't need me. And I'm not running away, I'm running *toward* life. The way out is the way in."

"Whatever that means."

"Out of the comforts of suburbia and this safe white-bread Walmart satellite dish life. Diving into reality."

"That sounds funny coming from you."

"Hfmph. You should take a tip or two. Learn to consider others, be altruistic. What are you going to do, stick around and keep killing grandmas and accordion players?"

"Shh! You know about that???"

"I may be imaginary but I'm not a fool."

"Have you been spying on me?"

"You've left more bread crumbs behind you than you think."

"What are you saying?"

"I'm saying that it wouldn't be too hard for the police around here, if they didn't have their heads up their butts or their dicks in dead teenagers, to start piecing this all together. You might want to come up with an escape plan, like me. And/or atonement."

"Do you know about Po?"

"The new boyfriend? A little. How is that going?"

"All right. I think he might know about . . . you know."

"Maybe you should come clean."

"My god, no. It's only been a few dates."

"But you slept with him?"   Farza's cadence here suggested that he honestly did not know for certain if she had.

"That's none of your business. I'm 19. So what if I did? Does that automatically make things serious?"

"Maybe not.   But I do know that when people start slapping their sweaty bodies together, the soul is there, too. That makes things serious, no matter how much you think you can separate body and soul."

"Soul? I'm not even sure there is such a thing."

"Ha."   Farza got up, brushed off his knees, and repositioned himself on his scooter.   "You know, Descartes thought the soul was in the pineal gland, in the brain."

"The what?"

"The pineal gland.   It's a little doo-hickey in there. When Descartes was around, they had no clue what it did, so he surmised that it must be where the soul is. There must be soul, and we know it isn't here, so it must be there. Smart guy, that Descartes. Now we know that the pineal gland regulates the biological clock, stuff like that. No soul. Descartes was a shithead."

"So where is the soul?"

"Where isn't it?"

"I hate it when you're cryptic." Chelsea said with genuine frustration. "And since when do you give sermonettes?"

"Today. A parting gift just for you. Descartes lived during the religious wars and tried to make a run for it into this safe, imaginary world – the coordinate plane. Cartesian coordinates, x and y, remember that?"

"Sure. From Algebra class."

"I suggest you head the other direction."

"Didn't he also say 'I think therefore I am'?"

"Right, obviously, he wasn't a musician or artist and never went dancing. Des-farts, if you ask me. Okay, darlin', I gotta go."

"Can I get a hug first?" Chelsea gently implored. Farza smiled. She stood up, and he gave her a hug and reached down and squeezed her ass for good measure.

"Hey!" she said.

"Something to remember me by. Pinched an inch. Never too late to start aerobicizing."

Chelsea sat back down and shivered and cried and ached. What was happening to her world?

♪ ♪ ♪

She stayed there like that for a while in a daze, who knows for how long. The campus buzzed around her, pulsating with the mechanical energy of routine. Another familiar voice lifted Chelsea out of her stupor.

"Hey, kiddo!" It was Carrie, all dressed in black and wearing sunglasses, the sun behind her.

"Hi."

"What gives? You just hanging out?"

"Yeah."

"Good for you. Sometimes we need to get sunburned just to feel alive, eh? Goddamn day," Carrie said as she sat beside her troubled friend, sipping from the ubiquitous water bottle. "So how is the love affair?"

"Oh, not much."

"Ha. This 'not much' doesn't sound like the other day's 'not much.' Any developments?"

"We made love."

"You sound less than enthused. How was it?"

'It was great, really, but something felt out of place."

"Literally?"

"No, I mean . . . I don't know. I guess it was just too soon."

"Did he, um, you know, in your face?"

"What?"

"You know, ejaculate in your face? Guys like to do that now."

"They do? Ick. No."

"Yeah, they pick it up from internet porn. Their idea of safe sex, here's mud in your eye, et cetera."

"That's disgusting."

"Hmm. So that wasn't the issue. Was he rough?"

"No, very loving."

"Okay, I see. Did Prince Charming kick you out after, make you do the walk of shame? That's an older guy thing. Have you seen him since?"

"It wasn't his idea, but I decided to leave that night, mainly because he didn't assume that I would stay."

"I can understand that."

"We had dinner with my mother yesterday. It was okay. But there's other stuff going on, too."

"Want to talk about it?"

"I need to figure it out myself first, I think."

"Fair enough. Well, since the Freudalizing will have to wait, I'd suggest we blow out of here and go do something fun, a suitable distraction to get our minds off of men and boys and books and crooks. Game? Unless you want to park it here all day."

"What did you have in mind?"

"Shoot some pool? Hit a movie? Hit a pool? Shoot some swimmers?"

"All of the above."

"You're on. Let's do it."

As they were walking away from the fountain, Carrie looked up at the sky and asked Chelsea, "Have you ever seen birds having sex?"

"No, have you?"

"They fit in the category of mounters. The male will jump on the female's back, wham bam."

"In the air, while flying?"

"I don't know, I don't see why not. If I were a bird I'd do it that way."

"So birds have penises?"

"Ducks and other waterfowl have wangs, not so much the other ones. I learned that in zoology class."

"I can't say I've ever seen a bird with a stiffy. What do the ones do that don't have penises?"

"I guess they figure it out."

♪ ♪ ♪

Po called in sick that morning, skipping work for only

204

the third time in a year. The previous occasions were due to (1) minor tonsillitis in mid-October and (2) a screaming hangover the morning after a bachelor party back in January. In the first instance, the doctor put Po on antibiotics and let him keep his tonsils. Po dragged himself to the office the rest of that week. In the second, a raspy-voiced thirty-something stripper had regaled the boys with some frightening, very intimate applications for hot candle wax, and Po kept drinking well past the tipping point trying to get those disturbing images out of his head. He woke up tasting bile and feeling like someone had planted a rusty axe in his forehead, wishing someone would finish the job and put an end to his misery. No combination of tylenol and pepto was going to right that ship, so he left a voice mail for his boss explaining the situation and climbed back under the sheets. Someone one time, he couldn't recall who, had advised for headache pain rapid breathing to increase oxygenated blood-flow to the brain. Supposedly it was a Hindu practice that reproduced the sensation of being in the mother's womb. Seeing how the tylenol just seemed to make the headache angrier, Po tried Hindu womb breathing until he fell back asleep, but his head still felt like it was in a vise. He really only started to feel better after he vomited. Kneeling on the cold bathroom floor, it occurred to him from the odor that his puke was almost pure alcohol, and he wondered, did hardcore drunks recycle their

205

purgings during Prohibition years?   Such is the level of commitment that addiction can inspire.

That was then, and Po again found himself wishing for a rusty axe or, better yet, a samurai sword — something simple and clean to rid him of these persistent, nagging thoughts about Chelsea. He couldn't help but think the unthinkable, running through it all over and over: *Nuts, the kid died of nuts. How did nuts get in his chili? Why did Chelsea have that bag of crushed peanuts? She never did explain it. Chelsea was with him when he died, there sitting at the table. He croaked right in front of her, and she barely seems to care about it. But she couldn't have done it. Intentionally? Impossible. No way. Maybe, but why? Why would she do such a thing? What possible reason could there be? Is it all just a coincidence? Is that sweet girl a murderer? It must have been an accident. Or a coincidence. Does she love me? Do I love her? Does her mom want to fuck me? Would I fuck her Mom?* He stared at the living room floor where he and Chelsea had made love, and he felt a strong urge to rip up the carpet and throw it out the window, set his condo on fire, and then go to Alaska, the Amazon, Outer Mongolia, Norway, Patagonia, anywhere.

chapter twenty-four

matinee

Chelsea and Carrie went to a matinee, the latest frenetic Hollywood action film. In this particular one the twenty-minute car chase culminated with a BMW speedster crashing into a helicopter and the helicopter flying for a bit before crashing into a space shuttle being built by terrorists. Boom. A victory for the very American hero and thus democracy and humankind. Hooray. Carrie and Chelsea marveled at how shitty the acting was and how fast the cuts; the jerkiness was nauseating. "Complementary lobotomies in the lobby on the way out," Carrie said as they ascended the aisle, their shoes sticking to the accumulated syrupy goo. About that time orchestra practice was beginning with one empty violin seat.

Next stop was a pool hall for a half-dozen games of nine-ball. Carrie cursed as Chelsea defeated her five out of six, which meant that Carrie had to spring for dinner. They opted for the most festive and unhealthiest of cuisines, Mexican, and the biggest burritos they could find. Carrie raised her glass of horchata and made a toast: "Girls rock, boys can go to hell." Chelsea nodded and said, "Amen." She realized her cell phone had been off for hours and she had three messages from Jan Edwards, followed by two from her mother, and none from Po. It had completely slipped Chelsea's mind that Gerald's memorial service was next day, and that she had agreed to perform, *pro bono* no less. Ugh. Mrs. Edwards was calling to confirm and to discuss the song list. Her mother's messages were inquisitive nags about where Chelsea was, why she hadn't called back Mrs. Edwards, and so on.

"Shit, I'd better call her."

"Who?" Carrie asked, as the salsa slipped off her chip before she could get it in her mouth. "Damn."

"Gerald Edwards' mother. I'm supposed to play at the funeral tomorrow."

"Oh yeah, I heard about that. The chili boy. You know them?"

"He and I used to do the funeral gigs together. He was an accordionist."

"And now it's his turn to be serenaded. How ironic."

"I suppose."

208

"Hey, we're all going to get it sometime. It might as well be memorable. Something ridiculously unforgettable, a big to-do."

"I know what you mean. I think I'd rather die peacefully in my sleep."

"Not me. Trampled by a rampaging rhino, bitten by a cobra, stranded on top of Mount McKinley, heroin OD, sex-induced heart attack at age 85, that's more my style."

"All at once? That's a full day."

"Ha. Go make your call, I'll see if I can talk our way into some margaritas. They always card here, though."—

"I'll be right back."

Chelsea went outside to the sidewalk in front of the restaurant. There was a brisk, chilly, hard wind; it was 55 degrees at most. Spring was taking its sweet time settling in year. Chelsea took a slow breath and dialed Jan Edwards' number.

"Hi, Mrs. Edwards? It's Chelsea Walker."

"Oh, hi Chelsea. Thanks for calling back. I'm sorry about leaving so many messages. I need to make these arrangements."

"That's no problem. I was . . . in class."

"Right, I'm sorry, I forgot, you're in college. You can't have your phone ringing during lecture."

"How are you holding up?"

"Oh fine, it's not easy, but I think I've been too busy with everything to have time to fall apart, if you know what I mean. Family's been arriving all day today, my husband and I have been running around like chickens with our heads cut off trying to get everything done. Mr. Holling, the school principal, has been very nice, though."

"So the service will be at the high school?"

"In the main auditorium. The whole student body will be there."

"Wow."

"Family and friends of the family, plus local well-wishers will be in the first three rows."

"I see."

"I dropped off the tentative program with your Mom earlier. We'd like to play a few things before the eulogies, and then something special after."

"No problem. What songs?"

"At the beginning we were thinking a religious hymn, 'Nearer, My God, to Thee,' then at the end a medley of Gerald's favorite science fiction theme songs."

"Doctor Who?"

"*Doctor Who*, *Star Trek*, and *Star Wars*. Very slow, respectful, tender."

"Okay, I can learn those or dig up the sheet music."

"Thank you so much, Chelsea. I know this would have meant so much to Gerry."

Chelsea wanted so say something comforting and reassuring but mainly was thinking about getting back to her veggie burrito before it got cold. "This will be a lovely service, I'm sure, Mrs. Edwards."

"I think so. Well, I don't want to take up any more of your time. Gerald's grandparents are here and I really should go. Thank you again, Chelsea. Oh, can you be at the high school tomorrow at 9 am?"

"Definitely. You're welcome. Take care, Mrs. Edwards."

Chelsea went back in and sat down. The food had arrived and Carrie already started eating. "That was a downer," Chelsea said.

"How'd it go?" Carrie asked as she was chewing.

"The service will be at the high school, in front of everybody."

"No shit?"

"Looks like I'm the music. No English class for me tomorrow."

"What's on tap? 'Another One Bites the Dust'?"

"A Christian hymn, then the themes to *Doctor Who* and

211

Star Wars."

"Right on. Then they're going to shoot him into space?"

"Ah, he would have loved that."

"I'm not into the whole 'throw 'em in the dirt' idea."

"Me neither."

"Six feet closer to hell. I say bury me on top of a high rise, so the trip down takes longer. Your dude call?"

"Nope?"

"Hmm. Well, don't worry about it. He's probably getting fucked in the ass as we speak. His secret life, ha. You're better off without him."

"Maybe. Carrie, what's the strangest reason you ever broke up with a guy?"

"Strangest?"

"You know, least significant."

"Well, once I broke up with this dude because I caught him shopping at Walmart."

"Really?"

"Yeah, he said he bought dog food there because it was so much cheaper. A lame excuse."

"How did you catch him?"

"I was there shopping, duh. . . . but it wasn't about me, it was about him, and the principle of the thing. Hey, that burrito isn't going to eat itself. Mine's delicious."

212

It did look inviting. Chelsea dove in. Carrie had flirted successfully with the happy waiter who was now bringing two extra large margaritas, one blended and one on the rocks.

"Rodrigo, my hero!" Carrie said as she moved her plate to make room for the drinks. Even the usually crass Carrie knew that a little flattery with the opposite sex goes a long way. "The greatest waiter ever ever *ever,* in this or any other universe. Drink up, girlie!"

With his wife in Juarez visiting her mother, Rodrigo would lay in bed that night imagining both of them in his own little action movie. His restaurant never used squirrel meat but occasionally cockroaches would belly-flop into the menudo.

chapter twenty-five

so long, space captain

Chelsea stood on the auditorium stage in her nicest black dress, playing "Nearer, My God, to Thee." Directly to her left was Gerald "in state," as they say, in an open casket with his accordion on his chest. His parents decided it fitting that he be buried with it, which meant an oversized coffin. If it were a shoe it'd be a Triple E. Gerald's skin was hardly recognizable — beyond the normal mortician pasty pink embalming special, his zits had all been concealed, his hair washed, boogers scooped out and nose-hair trimmed. The kid wasn't half-bad looking all spruced up. It was a packed house — over 700 students (all wearing black armbands, some already going through the motions of crying), family members, and town dignitaries. Chelsea's mother couldn't get off work but did plan to make it later for the internment. Claude Boles tried to crash the service but was stopped at the door. He was starting to cause a commotion when Gerald's father looked back, saw what was happening, and pointed first sternly at Boles to leave and then secondly at the police officer who was present for security. Boles got the message and left meekly without further incident. He sincerely wanted to apologize in person to the family, however awkward it might be, but decided to wait for a less public occasion, especially since he was being unceremoniously bounced.

Chelsea played her violin with feeling and the hymn was warmly received. With the second verse many in the audience began singing along. It was rather beautiful. Chelsea herself felt tingly, close to tears, but mainly she was thinking of her father, of Po and Farza, not Gerald.

It turns out that Gerald and his family were Catholic, so Father McEleney was to be in charge of the memorial. He remembered Chelsea from the Rosenbaum service and said hello. After she finished playing the hymn, Chelsea was to stand in the back corner of the stage until the final sci-fi send-off. Positioned at the makeshift pulpit, Father McEleney thanked her then addressed the crowd.

"Friends, loved ones, fellow Christians, and others. We are here today to pay our last respects to a young man, a bright shining star, who has left our skies all too soon, and is now much nearer to thee, our dear God. Goodbyes will be said, including a tribute by Mayor Nettlegrass, followed by the reading of a few scriptures selected by the family. First will be a special performance by Guncho the clown, a local entertainer many of you know firsthand. Gerald, I am told, loved clowns, and Guncho appeared at all of Gerald's birthday parties, from age 3 to the most recent, 15." McEleney was interrupted by a loud wail from Mrs. Edwards, who was comforted by her husband. "So let us please welcome Guncho, who has taken time from his busy schedule to be with us here today."

Chelsea found it hard to believe what she was seeing. Guncho, in full clown make-up, oversized bowtie and floppy shoes, the works, rode a tricycle onto the stage, doing laps around the coffin and ringing the bell on the handlebar as if to ward off evil spirits. He then leapt off into a cartwheel, ending up right at the microphone, pressing the button that made his bowtie spin. Known for his gymnastics, magic tricks, and weakness for pot smoking, Guncho also never talked during his act, preferring to mime. But now he opened his mouth (with a white-painted frown) to speak:

"Hi. I'm not a man of many words, but I just wanted to say that Gerald was a damn good kid. He always ate whatever cake and ice cream was on his plate; as far as I know, he hadn't pissed his pants at a birthday party since he was 9, and he never ceased being startled—and I mean downright scared—by balloon animals." He reached into his faux hobo bindle and pulled up a balloon giraffe, shaking it wildly. No one was sure whether to laugh. "But if I may be serious, ladies and gentlemen, my daughter, my little angel of a daughter, Sarah, died of leukemia when she was 6. For only six years did she grace this earth, six years she graced my life. I understand what it means to lose a child. It was when Sarah passed away that I decided to quit the post office and become a full-time harlequin, which is a fancy name for clown, to devote myself to making children happy, to giving them lasting memories. My daughter, god rest her soul, was short-changed and cheated, called too soon to become a memory, as has young Gerald. Let us never forget them. Let us never forget love."

Even the football jocks, who were in the back corner of the auditorium punching each other in the arm and secretly imagining sucking each other's cocks, couldn't help but be a bit teary-eyed. Mrs. Edwards visibly sobbed as Guncho's comments were met with strong applause. Chelsea looked shyly at Gerald's corpse and said to herself, *What next?*

Principal Holling climbed back up the stage to the rostrum and announced the next speaker, the 550-pound four-term Mayor of our fair city, Gustav Nettlegras. In addition to his sheer girth, Nettlegrass' distinguishing feature was a "skullet," — that is, a bald pate but with long hair in the back, like a mullet with a shine.

"Thank you, Principal Holling." Nettlegrass cleared his throat and tasted a hint of the double-stack of pancakes he had for his late breakfast and the two turkey subs he consumed for an early lunch. Mayonnaise and maple syrup. Generally, he liked to eat fried eggs on Friday, just because he liked the way it sounded, so that was on his agenda for the afternoon. "Friends, neighbors, students, citizens. It is always a sad occasion when we gather to bury one of our own, but it is especially troubling when it is such a young member of our community, one who had such a tremendous future ahead of him, and when his leaving us was so premature and so preventable. It was a terrible, terrible accident, just shameful. Maybe everything is all meant to be, but I don't think so. That's a lazy man's excuse. I stand here today to promise you all that your elected officials will do everything in our power, everything, to ensure that nothing like this will happen again. Life need not be chaos, if we work together and refuse to let it be. Death may be out there waiting for all of us, that's part of the order of things — but we can do our part, and should do all that we can, to see that it comes at the right time. That's the difference between us and the uncivilized. In the animal world, it's just predator and prey. Those cute freshly-hatched baby turtles on the beach crawl out of their sand nests and dart for the water, flailing all the way, hundreds at a time, we've all seen that on TV. For the seagulls, it's a buffet. They circle overheard and snatch one after the other. It's a senseless slaughter that seems cruel and unnecessary, even evil. But there's hope: a few turtles make it to sea and live long happy turtle lives, come back to the same beach later to nest, just like we all do, and the whole grand parade is repeated, even among the, ahem, political animals. Life, death, struggle, this is all part of God's plan, Father McEleney would tell us. Gerald didn't quite make it to the water, but, as my Buddhist friends would say . . ." Nettlegras paused and his eyes turned to the two Vietnamese teens in the audience, Thok and Nguyen, for dramatic effect. (Thok and Nguyen were new students who were uncomfortable enough to begin with, being minorities in this very white town as it was were, but they were doubly nervous in the corpulent Mayor's stare, as if they were his lunch.) " . . . Gerald has reached the farther shore. Thank you. My deepest condolences and very best wishes to the Edwards family."

There was a round of polite applause for the popular mayor. Chelsea continued to stand on the stage holding her violin in one hand and bow in the other, wishing she could dig a hole or find a trap door and jump in. Holling applauded as he leaned in to the microphone to introduce the next speaker, a student, Susie Goldfarb, a wispy, frail girl with straight blond hair and a large metallic structure on her face attached to her teeth that secured her braces. It glistened like a halo as she walked to the podium. Chelsea had never seen her before; she assumed she was a classmate and friend of Gerald's, but this was only half the story.

"Gerald Edwards and I were lovers," Susie said quietly, slurring her speech as a result of her dental apparatus. A collective gasp filled the room. Jan Edwards' mouth was agape and her husband had a shocked smile, a mixture of surprise and pride to learn that his son was "getting some," even from this girl who resembled a dog kennel crossed with a mop and the Eiffel Tower.

"Not in a sexual way, of course, given our age," Susie continued. Mr. and Mrs. Edwards in unison let out loud sighs, hers of relief, his of disappointment. " . . . but in a spiritual sense that was much more powerful and lasting. Very few of you knew Gerry except as that dork with the goofy laugh and poor hygiene, who was good at math, someone to make fun of, borrow homework from, shake down, terrorize, but he was my *friend,* and neither of us had very many. Friendships like that count more. We didn't take each other for granted, like so many of you do. He was a good person—kind, generous, pure-hearted, smart, hopeful. He had dreams, ideas for inventions, hobbies like music and comic books that he was so passionate about. He wasn't afraid to be who he was, no matter what people thought, he wasn't afraid to live, to laugh — that awful, shrill, joyous laugh of his." She started to cry, her voice tremble. "Although he died far too young, before he could realize his dreams, we all have so much that we can learn from him about how to live, how to be true individuals, how to love life, no matter how nerdy or geeky that might be sometimes. I wish you could have lived just a little longer, Gerry, to see my braces come off, to go to college, so more people could have appreciated the amazing person you were when you were alive, so we could have spent so many more wonderful moments together. I love you, and I'll miss you."

Susie slowly descended the stage. The silence was deafening, as was the common sense of shame. Chelsea was in tears, as was everyone in the auditorium who had a soul, which was a solid 79%. She wiped her cheek with her bow hand. *My God, what have I done?* Darlene was nowhere to be seen.

Holling asked his assistant principal if he knew anything about this sweet girl with the satellite dish on her head, and she said no. Gerald's father, Mitch Edwards, a manly-looking mortgage broker, was next to give a eulogy. He stood at the microphone, pulled index cards out of his inside suit pocket, stared at them, then put them back.

"I did have a few remarks written down, but I think it's best if I follow the example of this young lady, and Mayor Nettlegras, and of course Guncho, and speak straight from the heart. To be honest, I can't say that I knew my son all that well. He always seemed like a visitor from another planet to me, a stranger in our house, this weird exchange student from Jupiter. Gerald was on a very different wavelength than me, I guess from most of us. Jan, his mother, understood him better, and I give her credit for listening to him and so readily giving him the love and support that I should have, my share and then some. I played sports growing up—you name it, I played it—and Gerald would rather play the accordion or fantasy video games, rather drink Hawaiian Punch or Sunny D than a beer, didn't even want to try one at fifteen. And damn that kid loved cheetos and Danish butter cookies. I can't stand either. He had none of my interest in investment or business. I would be lying if I didn't say that I was disappointed that he wasn't a carbon copy of me, but what I also was, something I never told him, was that I was proud, proud to be his Dad. I admired his brain, his concentration, his musical ability, his imagination especially, his zest for living life on his own terms, which, uh, Susie"—he looked at the girl and smiled— ". . . described so well, things I never had. I mean, I have a brain," he laughed, and most of the audience did also, eager to release the tension that had been

222

steadily building over the last few speeches. " . . . allegedly, but not like his. No way. Gerald was so bright. The whole world was ready to open up to him. I was sure he was going to give Bill Gates a run for his money, be sitting up in some mansion someday soon with a harem of foxy babes draped over his accordion, rolling in money and computer parts, eating turkey legs and caviar. Maybe that's where he is now. But we're stuck down here without him, and now I am a father without a son, all because of little peanuts we've all eaten a million times. The smallest thing took my boy away. He's gone, I accept that, that's the way things go. No one said it would be a fair deal on this earth. But he will always be in my heart, I will see him in the mirror, and nobody can take that away. I don't know if there is a God or not, if he's like what's in the Bible or blue-skinned with twenty arms or whatever. My wife is more faithful than I am, and I admire her for it, but I just don't have it in me, never did. If there is a God, all I can say is, Gerry, son, give Him hell!!!"

With this there was raucous cheering from the students. Mitch Edwards lowered his head and shuffled off the stage, aware of the effect of his speech but numb to it. He felt like he had somehow channeled his old rough and ready high school football coach (sans the flatulence), but this was halftime to what?

Father McEleney followed with a few select passages

from the "good book," which is a funny expression considering that the state Driver's Manual is in many ways a better-written, livelier, more useful book. You'd think for the one true religion straight from God's cosmic lips we could get a "great" book. The basic gist of what McEleney read from Proverbs, Thessalonians and wherever, was that he who believes in Christ shall have life everlasting, be nestled in God's bosom on Judgment Day, which was apparently the place to be; this world ain't all that, the righteous need not fear death, since they aren't really dead or something along those lines, Jesus will look out for his homeys, blah blah blah. Chelsea wasn't impressed. Let's see the good Father dance with a chicken and raise Lazarus Jr., make Gerald hop out of the casket and stop all these good people from bawling. Now that would be a religion worth a damn.

After this was the processional and also when Chelsea was supposed to play the sci fi theme songs. She did so beautifully, tenderly, particularly the uplifting, trance-like Star Trek theme. First the family walked past the coffin to pay their last respects; the students lined up to do the same, as was the plan, but this was a very bad idea. While many of the kids were reverent and took the opportunity to reflect on death and say a touching goodbye to a classmate, others saw it as the opportunity for practical jokes. Someone put gum in Gerald's hair, for example; another thought it comical to place a jar of Planters peanuts next to him (word had gotten around the day before that it was the nuts and not the peppers that did young Gerald in); Justin Farrell, a senior, slapped a bumper sticker on the coffin that read "Honk if you're horny," while his friend Glenn Dent affixed one that said "I'd rather be sailing." It took the funeral director a solid forty-five minutes to scrape off the stickers, and not all the sticker shrapnel could be removed. When Principal Holling learned of the pranks, he was "mortified," as he put it, and gave the school a stern lecture over the PA on the following Monday, promising to suspend the culprits for a month, but they were never found.

chapter twenty-six
ebola joe

The internment was a more intimate affair, with just family members and close friends. Chelsea watched as the shiny purple casket—no cheap crate, she correctly deduced—was lowered into the ground, to be slowly broken down by the elements and insects over the years. She and her mother both lined up to sprinkle dirt on the coffin, as is the custom. Chelsea, who hadn't eaten all day, imagined it was ground pepper being sprinkled on a Japanese eggplant.

She gave her regards to Mr. and Mrs. Edwards, and told her mother that she was going for a walk and would be home later, leaving her violin with her. After wandering aimlessly for a time, Chelsea found herself at the 7-11 on the east side of town, still in her black formal dress, craving an ice cream sandwich. This made her think of Po. He hadn't e-mailed or called or anything since Wednesday, the night of the dinner. It was only Friday, but time—and silence—are amplified in such a situation. Chelsea still believed he might call, that he just needed some time to himself to sort things out, or that it was a natural pause or "blip" as she called it. You can imagine the sort of strain that suspicion of homicide can put on a fledgling relationship. Lounging peacefully at the corner of the building was Ebola Joe himself, the grizzled toothless Vietnam Vet, sun-baked and bone-thin, reeking of caked-on crud, stale urine, cheap liquor, and what seemed to be the odor of A-1 steak sauce and citronella. Combined, this was the unmistakable stench of *freedom*. His eyes were closed and he was humming to himself, his dog Snarf dozing serenely at his side. As Chelsea sidled past dog and human companion, circumventing the force-field of stink, Ebola Joe lifted his eyelids and spoke:

"Goin' to spend some of that money, young lady?"

Chelsea was surprised when he addressed her, surprised that he would do so in the first place and taken aback by his gravely, rural-sounding voice—not to mention the strange quality of the words themselves. "Uh . . . excuse me?"

"Ha. Yer gonna spend some of that hard-earned money, you been plugging away at that new job of yours . . . or should I say un-plugging away? And poppin' those pistachios where they don't belong? Ha."

Chelsea suddenly felt *seen.*

"Um . . . do I know you?"

"Now that's a tricky question. How'm I s'posed to know what you know . . . when it's hard enough knowin' what I know? I barely got a grip on any of it. I think!"

"It?"

Ebola Joe lifted his hands up towards his face and looked up momentarily, speaking in hushed tones. "The cosmos, all of it. No small thing to get a hold of. Catch a tigger by the tail, they say. More like catch the plague, ha . . . . Have a seat next to me, missy. Don't mind Snarf. He's planning to sleep through Armageddon."

He smiled warmly and patted the oil-stained concrete curb next to him. Chelsea paused for a moment then obliged, realizing that she would have to take this ride. The cool kids talk to homeless people, after all, thinking they are so rebellious but unable to conceal their paternalistic condescension. Chelsea was more down to earth and humble than that, and easily recognized Ebola Joe's wisdom and friendliness, edges and all—plus he seemed to know about her little moneymaking scheme. But how? And, man, he smelled so bad!

"Yer prob'ly thinkin' about my fumes. Doesn't take no Claire Voyeur to figure that out, ha . . . "

Chelsea wondered if he had howling winds in his head,

but he did his best to put her at ease.

"Really don't pay no mind to ol' Snarf here — he's got the mange but a heart of gold to go with it. No ordinary cur."

"So are you homeless?"

"You might say that, or you might say that the whole world's my home. It wasn't always like that. I used to saddle up the ol' rat like everyone else. It's expensive to live, I learnt that much, before the war and after, although during it ain't worth much. If you ain't got a mortgage, you got the rent, payin' off the car, insurance, always worryin' about the next day. But I had a thought back then, not long after I came back . . . what if you tell yourself you don't need a house and a car? What if you say I'm goin' to leave tomorrow to tomorrow? All my worries are today's. Some might call that freedom. And ain't nobody shooting at me anymore, or naggin' me, or pullin' the strings." He moved his arms around to illustrate the point, continuing his thought. "One day I woke up; the war was long over, but I could still hear them bullets, and I said to myself, 'Desire ain't what I want,' and I guess that was that. Game over. Not many people are at peace who fought in that war, thirty years later. Same with soldiers in every way, I guess. They got the mark of Cain, like me. But not many are at peace anywhere around here either. Or free, whatever it means."

"Are you free? Happy?"

229

"Ha . . ." He liked this girl, as he foresaw that he would. "Everyday is a choice, so I guess I like it well enough. When I'm tired I sleep, and when I'm not sleeping I'm awake. That's more than most folks."

"What do you eat?" Chelsea asked. She imagined the worst.

"Snarf here finds us food . . . he's a bit of a gourmet mutt, and then there are *charitable* donations," he winked. "We keep it fairly simple, though. I been hearing about ecological footprints, I read a bit about it — more like ecological butt prints, these fat asses all around. Not me, darlin'! A lean machine! My Daddy always said, 'don't trust a man shaped like a pear.' He was right." Ebola Joe smiled; Chelsea counted seven visible teeth, two of which were clearly rotting.

"What do you do all day long?"

"I ain't sitting at a desk in a dry wall box, I know that. A goddamn coffin. You know about those, ha. If the sun comes out, I'm here to see it, maybe the first to know. No, no robot dance for me. I sit and think, mostly, talk to people. I'm writing a book in my mind . . ." He made typing movements with his grimy fingers.

"What's it about?"

"It's a sequel to *all* of 'em. Somethin' better."

"A sequel to all books?"

"That's right. It's gonna be somethin'. Capital 'S.' You ever hear of the Cassandra Complex?"

It did sound familiar. "I think so. That's from Greek mythology?"

"Smart girl, yep indeed. Cassandra was one of them Trojan women . . . "

"From the Trojan War," Chelsea interjected, finding herself fascinated by Ebola Joe and wanting to impress him.

"Yep. Greeks snuck in that wooden hobbyhorse and burnt the city to the ground. Cassandra was a prophet, a girl, who could see into the future—who knew Fate, knew it like the back of her hand, like when you close yer eyes at night that's what she saw, except it was the future, and all day long. And you know for the Greeks Fate was fixed, like it all had been played out already. Cassandra was watchin' it like a movie. She got on Apollo's bad side, though, and he cursed her . . . whiz-bam! So that even though she could see the future, could see it all, no one would ever believe her."

"I remember, she would warn people . . . "

"And they thought she was crazier'n a loon on Friday. It didn't help that she was a woman in ancient Greece. Maybe that was the curse. She'd still try to help them, though, what else could she do? I got a little of her in me. I also have a little bit of the Cass Elliott Complex, you know that one?"

"No. Is that Greek too?"

"Ha, maybe . . . she was a singer in the '60s, a group called the Mamas 'n' the Papas. A real belter. Mama Cass. Big as a house. A heart to match, supposedly. Mama Cass with her big fat ass. One day she tried to eat a footlong sandwich sideways and choked and died." He chuckled at his own way with words.

"Seriously?"

"They were all dying like that back then. Chokin' on their vomit, chokin' on someone else's vomit, chokin' the chicken like ol' Nero, swimmin' in sin, drownin' in drugs, turnin' blue, twenty arms all in the wrong places. I learnt somethin' from ol' Mama Cass, though . . . gotta learn to take smaller bites, chew, or even better, don't think of food as the cure for all. There ain't no cure for pain except strength and love. Maybe she's in Hades learning, or forever rollin' her lunch up a hill."

Chelsea thought about this. She could hear the winds and wanted to change the subject. "You don't have any family at all?"

"We're all family, you'll see." He looked down between his angular legs at his ragged shoes, his tone temporarily somber. "I had one, like everybody else, all dead now or run away. My Daddy was religious . . . Mormon. He thought Utah

232

was the Promised Land. Sounds more like a threat to me! I figgered that out even when I was a lil' snapper in the fields. He used to say the definition of a pervert is someone who has more things going into his ass than a-comin' out! Ha. He wasn't exactly right about that, but it's true that little kids are starvin', their stomachs growlin', and grown men are in the hospital because they done shoved things in their keysters and got 'em stuck! Kitchen tools, wildlife, you name it! And this is god's world!" He said this in such a funny way that Chelsea and he both laughed uncontrollably until their jaw muscles and spleens ached.

"You have a great sense of humor," Chelsea said admiringly.

"Aw, a sense of humor is just somethin' to survive. A kind of intelligence. Maybe the only real kind. But definitely a blessin'. . . one of them blessins we give to ourselves."

"You know . . . " Chelsea mentioned slowly, as if she were swallowing fire. "If you cleaned up and got a job, maybe people would believe you."

Ebola Joe smiled warmly. "Nah, ain't worth it! Ha. I got some bigger fish to fry. And so do you, eh?"

She dropped the subject and decided to mention what was on her mind. "So you know about . . . "

"I know." He fixed his eyes on her. "I killed my share

of folks in the war. My soul is still dirty from that. Now, you an' I both know that there are some people in this world who ain't worth a rusted dime — in fact, they just take other people's dimes. Take, take, take, then take some more. Give nothin' but grief back and sour looks, poisonin' the world. Cancer on skates. They ought to have mercy on us and die. Mercy dyin'! I don't have a problem with what you been doin'. It don't mean much to me. At least not the how, no-how. But you should think more on the *who*, maybe — folks who deserve it. Maybe they deserve it because they are good, maybe they deserve it because they are bad. You can't just be pullin' any ol' plug just 'cause you can. What do you call it, overnight shippin'? Ha. Maybe there ain't no point to nothin', but it's up to us make one — a good one."

Chelsea thought she understood. "And what about Gerald?"

"Ah, the boy with the squeezebox and the girlfriend with the birdcage on her head? Well, I guess he had a weak constitution. That wasn't very neighborly of you, now was it? But maybe some of what that preacher said is true, that no one dead is really dead, just invisible, gone fishin' for a while until Judgment Day."

"So is there a god?"

"Beats me. I guess Gerald's finding out, and we will too someday. Or not."

"I don't know anything anymore."

Ebola Joe raised his eyebrow and smiled. "Now we're getting somewhere. Yer all right by me, Chelsea. You know you ain't god, just a girl who plays violin who tries to get along in the world. But you're an artist, too—" He pronounced it *artiste,* with high affectation. "—and that means something. You git points for style, whether someone is keepin' track or not." He started pantomiming violin movements and humming the Blue Danube blissfully to himself, stopping after a few seconds, as if a ghost whispered in his ear. "There has to be somethin' deeper. Who's the audience? Is there an audience? Up there? Just us? Just me? Ah, who knows. All I can say is don't expect to change, don't expect *not* to change, and don't expect to remember this. The cosmos is like an ocean; the waves will come and the waves will go, and rain will fall on the waves, some of them cute lil' green sea turtles'll get snatched by the gulls, some'll swim and live for a hundred years, like that fat mayor said, ha, I bet he's eaten a few hisself. . . . I remember standin' at the ocean in Vietnam, in my boots, grenades hanging from my shirt, just listening. That was a sight, death all around and so much life. Maybe that's the definition of beauty."

The two shared a lengthy silence as these words sank in.

"So you can see the future?"

"Ain't nobody can see the future. It's hard enough

seeing the present. That's all I do. The past, shit, that's nothin' but a hangover. Easy enough to feel that. But the future, the best we can do is make guesses about it. Some folks are more tuned in than others. Some got their heads fully wedged up their own poop chutes, if not other things, like my daddy said. They're lucky if they can hear their own heartbeat, you know what I mean?"

Chelsea asked Ebola Joe, "Can I play you a song sometime?"

"Heh . . . you already have. I been hearin' it for a while. Tra-la-da-di-da! Go git yer ice cream and grab me and Snarf one too. Something expensive. No chocolate for him, though." The mutt woke up, pricked his ears, and raised his head for a second as if to say, "goddamnit shut up!" He nuzzled his chin back down onto the cement next to Ebola Joe's tattered pant leg and went back to sleep.

chapter twenty-seven

jenny revisited

After scrounging in the freezer case for suitable frozen delights, Chelsea paid the South Asian teen at the register and stepped through the automatic doors of the mini-mart. She was astonished to see Jenny Andrews, her unexpected benefactor, excitedly walking toward her, deep in thought, wearing the same outfit as their first meeting.

"Mrs. Andrews?"

Jenny's face came alive. "Why, Chelsea, honey! Now whoever told you to call me that! Let me give you a kiss!" It was comical how they both steered their bodies to avoid smooshing the ice cream that Chelsea held in both hands. Chelsea glanced over at Ebola Joe, half-expecting him to have vanished like Zeus in disguise (in Greek mythology this is known as the "Zeus Poof"), but nope, there he was. Snarf was now fully awake and eating what appeared to be kibble out of Ebola Joe's hat. Ebola Joe stopped concentrating on his dog for a second and smiled over at Chelsea, with a mien that said, "Don't ask, don't tell."

"So you're out of the home?" Chelsea asked Jenny.

"Making a break for it, my dear! Picking up supplies for the road," she confided with a wink. "I've never felt better in my life, to be honest. I love this fresh air!"

Not far from where they were standing was an over-filled dumpster and the stench wasn't exactly daisies and petunias. Chelsea raised her eyebrows and made a face.

"Well, you know what I mean, Chelsea! It's the aroma of life! Freedom!"

"Are you okay? Should I call the home?"

"No, no, no—don't you dare! I'd never forgive you. And nothing should take priority over ice cream, not if I have anything to say about it."

This time Chelsea looked over and Ebola Joe was gone. Chelsea's mouth hung open in disbelief. The next move was clear. "Hmm . . . would you like one?"

"I would love one! I thought you would never ask. Let's walk over to the park. I want to hear birds chirping and children playing. Such a lovely day! And pretty girls like us shouldn't be alone."

And so they ambled over and found a bench.

♪ ♪ ♪

The most famous and oft-visited city park in the United States is, of course, New York City's Central Park, named after its multi-millionaire benefactor, Bedford L. Central. The *L* stands for Lamont, of the Lamont Dry Cleaning, Boxcar, Gyroscope, and Sleeping Powder empire. Landscape Architect Elmer Armstead's vision for the park was of a bucolic escape from all the horses (over 200,000) and horseshit (over 700,000 pounds daily) that choked the streets of mid-19th century New York. The existing working-class neighborhoods were razed and the locals displaced to make room for paradise. Labyrinthine hiking trails were carved out of mountains of bituminous coal. To attract big-spending anglers, the park's reservoirs were stocked with large-mouth bass and mermaids — the mermaids being teenage Danish and Swedish immigrant girls who proved less hardy and aquatic than they indicated on their job applications. The mermaids drowned and the bass succumbed to an epidemic of malaria and typhus, courtesy of the infamous "Typhoid Mary," notorious fish-kisser, in the latter instance and "Malaria Fred" in the first. Originally the park had a fifty foot-high fence made out of soap and barbed wire (invented for the purpose) to keep out Catholics and the occasional Presbyterian ruffian. Central Park is located in the very far northernmost southeast corner of the island of Manhattan, the jewel of New York's Five Boroughs. The other four boroughs are Brookline Glacier (pronounced glai-jaw), West Serengeti, Queensfjord (including Flushing Meadows, site of the world's largest annual plumbing convention), and ritzy Stankin Island, home of New York's elites, the so-called Brahmins of Zion. Central Park is cordoned off by ultra-upscale Park Avenue, named after Korean investor Ghee Rho Park. Presently Central Park is home to over five hundred delightful species of endangered plant and animal life, such as the poisonous Periwinkle Daffodil, the majestic Methane Elm, the Bolivian Blue-tailed Hexapede, the left-handed New Jersey Spotted Mongoose (with only fifteen known right-handed ones in the world), the omnivorous Umbala Snot Lizard, and the iconographic Mount Vernon Wigger which also appears on the city's crest. In its rich history the park has been the locale for numerous performances of Shakespearean plays, countless gang rapes of woodland creatures, and several assassination attempts of hot dog vendors. Simon and Garfunkel reunited for a concert with the Bay City Rollers in Central Park in 1982, an event witnessed by well over 17 people.

While there are several competitors, the title of America's "Second Finest" or "Sub-Ultimate" urban park would likely have to be Golden Gate Park in San Francisco, which, contrary to the popular myth so rarely dispelled, is actually mostly green and consists of more than just a gate. Golden Gate Bridge, which connects the park to Saucilito's Giant Redwoods to the north, actually has three and a half gates and is painted a shimmering golden red, like the color of a gold brick after it has been used to bludgeon a rival prospector to death. Golden Gate Park was originally built with a fifty foot-high fence to keep the Chinese out and the queers and squirrels in. Fun trivia: there have been an estimated three hundred completely intact fossilized hippie skeletons discovered in the park since 1965, as carbon dating of their bandanas and blue jeans has confirmed.

♪ ♪ ♪

The park in which Jenny and Chelsea now found themselves seated had no such lofty claims to nobility. It was just a dinky space with a playground, unattractive splinter-filled benches, some halfway decent shade trees, and a less than pleasant view of the sewage treatment facility. But it was a peaceful sanctuary nonetheless. A plaque near the entrance on DeKalb Avenue marked the park's founding on May 15th, 1907. The town fathers couldn't afford to construct a fifty foot-high fence, opting instead—in a bitterly contested decision that threatened to consume the small city in the municipal equivalent of a Civil War—to devote that portion of the budget to sod and a blue swing set. Acid rain caused the disintegration of the original swing set in 1978, but its replacement has ably stood the test of time since. A little red-haired girl with pigtails and a white dress was at that moment swinging happily and had captured the attention of both Jenny and Chelsea.

"Such a cute little girl . . . but what kind of mother would send her daughter off to play in the grass and mud in a brand new white dress?" Jenny wondered.

"It does create a mood of suspense!"

"True, it's not whether she will be defiled but when. I wonder if she even has a mother."

"Doesn't everyone have a mother?"

"Theoretically. But not all mothers are equal, Chelsea. Oh, but look at her. This is heaven."

"Maybe." Chelsea felt guarded, unlike in her religious conversations with Carrie.

"No, this is it. Either she doesn't know what is coming, or she doesn't care."

"It's not guaranteed that she will ruin the dress."

"I suppose not. More power to her. Innocence is over-rated, but I miss it."

"You?" Chelsea was surprised by what she perceived to

be the implications of this.

"A woman's happiness is not a little girl's. It's heavy. A momentary forgetting of burdens at best, but they're never far away. Baggage!"

"I like to people watch. I like to try to imagine the burdens."

"Ah, me too! The challenge, I'd say, is to not be anywhere else, to engage in pure observation—although that sounds scientific, it's the complete opposite!"

"I think I understand."

"You do!" Jenny turned her face toward Chelsea and smiled. "I miss this. I could sit here forever." Just then a pigeon came very close to Chelsea's leg. "You have a friend, I think."

Chelsea checked her pockets for who knows what, and the ice cream was already long gone. "I wish I had something to give them! Oh wait!" She then automatically reached in her purse for the bag of crushed nuts that she had forgotten was no longer there. "Right. Ah, no, nothing to give them."

"Shh . . . pigeons always get their lunch, my dear, I wouldn't worry. But you have a kind heart." Jenny rested her hand tenderly on Chelsea's arm.

"My mother calls them rats with wings!"

"Gutter birds, we used to say! Pests. But all God's creatures, I suppose—or the most god-like, maybe, ha! Living off of our garbage."

Chelsea wasn't sure she could laugh, but Jenny's tone of voice communicated that everything — *everything* — was fine.

"Can I ask you something, Jenny?"

"Certainly, my dear."

"Why did you add me to your will?"

"Hmm. Why do you think?'

"I don't know, are you lonely?"

"Who isn't? Aren't you?"

"I suppose, sometimes. I thought I had found someone."

"Oh, there are plenty of someones, Chelsea, don't worry. Putting you in the will was impulsive, I admit, but it felt right. My son thinks I'm crazy, that I'm cheating my grandsons out of their birthright, but it's not that much money. Just enough so that you'll know."

"Know what?"

"Why, that there is love in the world, of course, and hope, and. . . "

"And little girls on swing sets?"

"Exactly! Don't you remember that feeling of the air kissing your face? Wanting to go higher and higher, but afraid of falling off? Wondering if the boys were staring up your dress! Laughing, screaming just for the h-e-l-l of it, wishing you could throw that awful violin teacher in the lake? Feeling so strangely old, as if you had already lived a thousand lifetimes, wanting to leap off at the very top and fly away?"

It was at that moment, when Jenny articulated every thought that Chelsea had ever had as a child on a swing, that she knew she was speaking to a ghost.

chapter twenty-eight

headlock

Back at the mall where we began, Chelsea was still reclining in the plastic arboretum (plastoretum?) near the fountain, now thinking mainly of Po, what she might have done differently, hoping he might call. Mrs. Andrews had left her $15,000, but Chelsea didn't care. She gave it to her mother to put in the college and general expenses fund. She started picturing the money in a pile, spraying it with lighter fluid, setting it ablaze, throwing her violin on the top. Just then, her cell phone rang. Laying on her back, she held the phone over her face up over her face, and disappointedly saw from the caller ID screen that it was Carrie.

"Hi Carrie."

"Hey Chels. Guess what?"

"What?"

"I've got a Christian in a headlock." Carrie had at long last had another run-in with the Christian girl who had thrown the mulch at her, and now had the poor little martyr in a vice grip worthy of an amateur wrestler. Chelsea could hear the captive's groans as she attempted to break free and was increasingly turning blue. Carrie was much stronger, however. "Turn the other cheek now, you Bible-thumping bitch." This was bordering on a hate crime. Carrie wasn't going to let her go until she renounced her Lord and Savior.

"Don't really hurt her, Carrie."

"I'll take a picture and send it to you when I'm done. What are you doing?"

"Oh, I'm locked in the mall."

"Right on. Well, have fun. Back to work for me. Talk to ya later."

Chelsea sighed and dropped her arms down. Instantly, the phone rang again. Assuming it was Carrie, Chelsea just began talking. "Did she pass out? Escape?"

"Huh? Excuse me?" It was Po. He couldn't believe what he was hearing and was already regretting the call.

"Po! Oh, I thought it was Carrie." Po knew enough not to ask for details.

"Sorry I haven't, um, called in a while."

"It's okay," she lied.

247

"Look, this awkward, but I think, um, we should . . . you know, cool it for a while."

Chelsea didn't want to speak. *I thought it had already cooled and died.* "I see." *Pumped and Dumped.*

"You do?"

"It's my age, isn't it?"

"N-no . . . although that doesn't make things easier."

"You know, girls mature faster than boys."

"Trust me, I know that. It's just that you might be, um, uh, a murderer. That's a bit difficult for me to deal with."

"I don't know what you are talking about."

"The accordionist?"

"It could have been the peppers. Either way, it did the world a favor."

"Please, don't try to rationalize this. And what have you been doing in those nursing homes? Just playing violin? Mrs. Andrews is dead."

"I had nothing to do with that. And everyone has baggage. Don't you? I never asked about the women you've been with."

"Yeah, true, but they're all still alive."

"So you called to say goodbye?"

"I don't know. Maybe. I need some time alone to think. You made me very happy."

"Me too."

"But what if that was all a lie?"

"Do you think it was?' Chelsea felt herself crying and her voice was beginning to crack.

"No."

"Neither do I. Even though you ordered pad thai."

"Huh?"

"Nothing. I don't want to lose you."

"I know there's something magical and beautiful between us, but I just don't think I know who you are."

"I'm *me*."

"I'm not saying it's over, but I need to think about things."

"What can I say?" Chelsea knew that thinking and love don't mix. This was the end, no matter what he might say.

"I'm sorry, Chelsea, I need to go. Are you at home?"

"No. The mall."

"Shopping?"

"No, it's closed."

Po could wonder what crimes she might be up to now. "I should go," he said.

"I know. I miss you."

"I miss you, too. Bye, Chelsea."

And that was that.

chapter 29 (epilogue)

the end of the affair

Boles never recovered from the chili disgrace and sold the restaurant for a fraction of its value. It is now a T.G.I. McWhatever. His dreams of holding political office all fizzled, of course, and he became little more than a bicycle shorts-wearing hermit. Riding a wave of public safety hysteria, Gustav Nettlegrass was elected to an unprecedented fifth term. He had his stomach stapled and lost 300 pounds in hardly any time at all. Meanwhile, peanut-related deaths in town were reduced to zero. The police never managed to connect the dots, never suspected Chelsea in Gerald's death or any of the deaths at the retirement homes, but continued to give unwarranted speeding tickets and bust underage drinkers. The police didn't get any help from Po, who quit the law firm, moved to Portland, entered a seminary after finding Jesus somewhere, and decided to never again play with sock puppets. He hit rock bottom when he was out of bread one day and found himself in his apartment eating hot dogs on hamburger buns.

Farza, meanwhile, made a real difference in the imaginary Peace Corps in Africa, much more than the real Peace Corps ever will. Darlene decided to take a vacation and hang out with him in Senegal, but not being properly immunized she caught a case of shoulder typhus and died. Chelsea's Aunt Amy continued to whiff with the guys, until one day she met . . . Ebola Joe, who had anticipated her coming, groomed himself for the occasion, and said all the right things. He moved in to her place and she started supporting him, keeping him and Snarf supplied with Ripple wine and ice cream.

Carrie spun in circles for a time, called people names, got some more tattoos, collected a few more loser boyfriends, and even "dabbled" with a Christian lesbian chick from her economics class. Videos of their close encounters can be found on the internet.

The new drugstore, two stories high of brick face and/or stucco, is open and doing fab business. Chelsea went to Russia with the orchestra, found St. Petersburg to be "dank and morose," and started dating an oboist. The two made beautiful music together for several weeks before she got tired of listening to his snoring at night and became generally bored with his mannerisms. The old folks missed her violin and bright smile. As for the express shipments, well, Chelsea doesn't think about any of it much anymore. It's an increasingly distant past. Meanwhile the "parcels" continue to pile up for God, who again laughed so hard that it rained shit.

Whatever other characters haven't been mentioned here, including all the various extras, hooked up with each other or interacted in some other very meaningful way, forming an impressive Celtic knot.

Or not.

♪

ABOUT THE AUTHOR

Royce Grubic is an author, songwriter, and artist currently living in Silver City, New Mexico. He has taught writing, philosophy, history, religious studies, and ethics at the University of Southern California (where he earned his doctorate), Washington State University, and Western New Mexico University. He has a long work of non-fiction called *Cosmos, Chaos, and Process in Western Thought: Towards a New Science and Existentialist Social Ethic* and a soon-to-be published second novel, *sNOweYES*. A sampling of his various creations, including the "misinforum" humor page, can be found at gorilladogmusic.com, the website named for his beloved pooch.

Made in the USA
Charleston, SC
14 December 2011